The Write

Way to Heal

Joshua Bovill and Rodrekous Hunter

Editing by Karolyn Herrera, DocEditing.com

"To escape is to feel
and to write is to live."

Carrie R. Bovill

1

Deon Sanders

A phrase that people have said every day never really applied in my hood. "When life gives you lemons, make lemonade." I guess it took guts to apply it because where I was from, people haven't lived by that. A more fitting analogy was, "When life gives you lemons, complain and eat them how they are because you are afraid to make something sweet out of them to balance it out." My name is Deon Sanders and despite being named after the NFL legend and Hall of Famer, I'm not a football player— I'm a poet.

A POOR MAN'S CRY
Before my mom had the finances to birth me,
  I was already born economically cursed,
  cursed since my poor, innocent birth
Sixteen years and yet I'm a living recession
Many blessings, still—I AM The great depression
Should I hang my head low? And wallow in my
  poverty?

Give in to the devil's grief and lose all
  sovereignty?
Should I just throw in the towel and use my
  financial disability as a crutch?
Cause the weight of the world is on my
  shoulders and it just weighs too much.
I could do all of these things but instead I
  will stand tall
I will get up like a man, no longer will I crawl
They say you can tell a lot from a man whose
  back is against the wall...
Well here I am devil—put on ya gloves, it's
  time to brawl
You may think I'm weak but I'm not gonna die
These are simply just my thoughts, a poor
  man's cry.

I closed my notebook to get ready for dinner.

"Deon! Make sure you get your dirty school clothes ready. I'm going to the laundromat after dinner," my mom yelled.

I went to the corner of my small, damp room to get the school clothes I'd folded up earlier. I walked into our tiny kitchen and set the table for Mom.

"What are we having?" I asked.

She smiled at me to indicate that it was something good. "Mac and cheese, ham, and peach cobbler and ice cream for dessert," she said.

Mom got out her oven mitts to put on her strong, tiny fingers. She placed the food on the old, wooden table. She then took off the mitts and sat at the table with me.

"Shoot God a prayer for us, baby," she said.

I grabbed her hands and said grace. We both said, "Amen." Mom then took out a knife to cut the ham. She hated quietness at the table, so we usually talked about anything and everything. I couldn't even front, she was my best friend.

"So, what's new at school, D?" she asked without looking up.

"It's aight. I'm trying to get them Cs up right now," I said, while putting a chunk of mac and cheese on my plate.

My mom gave me an encouraging nod because she knew I wasn't that great at school. It didn't matter how hard I tried, I just felt like I couldn't really get into any subject at school.

"Do you have to work tonight?" I asked.

She nodded with a disappointed look. I hated that look on my mom's face because it signified struggle, troubles, and pain. "Mom, you think we will ever get out of this place and somewhere a little bit better one day?" I asked.

She gave me an optimistic look. "Of course, because I believe you will go far. Now eat up so we can go to the laundromat."

I ate quickly and grabbed the bag of dirty clothes. After walking out, Mom locked the door. She always told me that locking the door was the difference between living and dying. Trust me; in my neighborhood, that was not a joke.

Right across the street from us was a plaza. Starting from left to right, it had a barbershop and salon, a liquor store, a convenience store, and a laundromat. We saw a few guys hanging around the liquor store who looked like they were in their thirties. One of the guys who was barely holding onto his teeth, was telling a story about his weekend and resenting the fact he had to clock in to work in the morning.

"Man I tell ya, my boss be tripping man. He said he gonna give me a point because I was six minutes late," I overheard him say. Points in a factory job were not a good thing.

We walked into the laundromat and saw Julie. Julie was two years older than me and had an amazing shape, short hair, and the face of a superstar. She was in school for cosmetology, but everybody said she needed to be a model.

"Hi, Ms. Sanders, hey D, how are y'all doing?" she asked, smiling and showing her dimples.

"Fine, Julie, how are you?" my mom asked.

"We are doing just fine, Ms. Sanders. Hope y'all are having a lovely evening," Julie replied, as she walked to the door to leave with her boyfriend, Nathan. I couldn't stand that dude.

My mom looked at me and whispered, "Now that boy know I don't like him. He need to go on somewhere with his highwater pants," she joked.

"Yeah, he need to sag; look like he's about to be out of breath in a minute with those pants," I said.

We both laughed out loud and noticed them looking at us, trying to get the joke. We stopped and continued washing clothes. Nobody liked Nathan because he was a spoiled guy who thought he could do whatever he wanted. He was one of those guys who got the best Christmas present in the world, and still complained about it. Another reason was because he was lame. He believed that his drip was impeccable, but his clothes hardly ever matched.

After we finished washing and drying our clothes, we headed back to the apartment.

As we settled back in, I put my school clothes in a drawer then opened my notebook to an empty page. I tried to think of something to write about. Damn—writer's block. I turned the lights off and went to bed.

When I dreamed, I had amazing dreams of what I wished my life were like. Usually, my dream centered around my mayo-colored Benz and a beautiful girlfriend that resembled a young Kim Kardashian. In this dream, people all around were snapping pictures of me, asking questions. Yeah, this was truly the life I deserved. I woke up in the middle of it and checked my beat-up flip phone to see what time it was. Only 4:38 a.m. I got up and took a shower. I always thought about taking long showers but couldn't. My shower had to last no longer than three minutes or the water would shut off. I put all the soap on and rinsed off very quickly.

After I dried off, I looked at myself in our rusty, cracked, but adequate mirror. It didn't matter how many haircuts I got, I still thought I was just a skinny, ugly kid. I put on my school clothes and cooked eggs, bacon, and pancakes for my mom. She usually came home at six in the morning. I always left early because I had to meet with my friends. I waited till about 5:30 then left. With my mom, I was known as a momma's boy but with my friends...it was just a different me, I guess.

We always met each other at "the spot" at six. Usually I was the first one there. It took me fifteen minutes to walk to the spot which usually gave me ten to twenty minutes to be alone and think for a while. I arrived at the spot at 5:50 and to my surprise, the crew was already there.

"What's up, bro?" said Mickey.

Out of everybody, Mickey was the most active. We called him Mickey because he was a very animated dude. He also had a lot of girls getting at him. Word had it that he'd almost got Julie to do *you know what* with him, but he told us it was just a rumor and he wouldn't disrespect her in that way. Plus, just looking at him, anyone could tell he was full of life. Then there was Jamal and Janie, brother and sister. Jamal was one year older than Janie but she seemed to act older. Jamal was a very playful individual which—for his size—made it hilarious. Jamal was about five foot eight and 240 pounds. His sister, on the other hand, was shaped nicely. Janie just had that radical appearance. She seemed like she just went to school without a care in the world. She'd never been on a date, and never been seen with a guy. She just hung with the homies.

"Deon, want to smoke this joint with us real quick before school?" Janie said.

I shook my head and said, "No." I'd tried smoking when I was thirteen. No particular reason, I just did it because my friends said it would help me relax. It didn't work for me, so I just wrote in my journal when I was stressed. Whenever my friends smoked, we would start talking about crazy stuff. Sometimes we talked about get-rich-quick schemes and sometimes we talked about life from a philosophical point of view.

"We should rob somebody," Mickey said.

Jamal looked at him skeptically. "You have to make sure they got money though," he replied.

"No, forget that. We need to start a business together," I interjected. I always believed that getting money the legal way was the way to do it because nobody could just randomly take your money. Selling drugs could be cool and I would do it to make a few dollars but if you owned a business and got that Oprah money, nobody could stop you.

"That's a good idea, D," Janie said as she took a hit off the joint. "I mean, entrepreneurs are already risktakers; might as well do it the clean way because nobody can tell you nothing," she continued.

"Man, y'all trippin'. Dope boys get way more respect than those white boys," Mickey said.

"Drug dealers got a better chance of going to jail than a person like Oprah, bruh," Jamal said.

"Whatever man. Y'all just don't know how to make money," said Mickey. After they finished the joint, we walked to school. If we took the bus, it would take us five minutes to get there but we usually walked. "Hey, did you read that Frederick Douglas bullshit for class?" Mickey asked.

"Yo man, that ain't bullshit, that's a part of our history, dummy," Jamal said, sternly.

"Yeah Mickey, that's not even funny. What you think about it, Deon?" Janie asked as she stared at me.

"I mean, he can believe in whatever he wants. If he don't think the book is good, then that's his opinion," I replied.

"Well, I hope y'all did y'all projects because mine's going to blow all of y'all's projects out the water," Jamal said, as he pulled out a flash drive from his bookbag.

"What's on it?" I asked.

He looked at it for a few seconds. "It's a video. It has pictures and a heartbreaking song on it. Man, I pray this is the right one," he said.

Janie grabbed it out of his hands. "Hmm, yeah, because I remember it being in the computer while you was working on it," she said.

"Damn, I forgot my project," said Mickey. We all looked at him with troubled looks.

"You know this is fifteen percent of our grade bro, you need to get on the ball," Jamal said.

"You need to just shut up, with yo' meatball-sub head," Mickey fired back. We all started to laugh hysterically. "I'm just kiddin'. I had this girl do like a book report thing for me. I paid her ten dollars."

I wondered how people were going to respond to my project. I hoped they were ready for a poem because this would be my first time reading one out loud.

"We going to hit the store before school because I want to see Julie," Mickey said.

"Hold up, she work at Lomart now?" Jamal asked. Mickey nodded and we walked in that direction. Lomart is the place where you can find everything you need. The best part about it was that it was right across the street from the school.

We walked in and saw Julie on the first register. "What's up, y'all, welcome to Lomart," she said, smiling and showing those perfect dimples.

"Baby, why you working here? I thought your man could take care of you better than that," Mickey said.

"Well, we took a little break," she said with a sad look.

Wow, that was fast! I just saw them at the laundromat last night. Something clearly went wrong in a short amount of time. I decided to keep my mouth closed though because it wasn't none of my business. After Mickey's conversation that didn't go anywhere, we decided to leave and head to school. It was 7:30 and class started at eight, so everybody was probably in the courtyard talking and roasting each other.

Janie gave me a playful smile. "I saw the way you be looking at Julie, bruh. You should talk to her or something because she might be interested," she said. Mickey gave her a snarling look.

"That's my girl and y'all know that—no discussion," he said.

I didn't know why Janie did that. She was lucky I didn't call her out. She's lucky she was my other best friend.

2

Mickey

"Eat something, Mickey," Ms. Brown said to her son. He was twelve, attending his uncle's funeral, watching everyone in sadness, grieving about a guy who helped his family and was also known in the streets. Mickey didn't know how to feel. He hadn't been that close to him, but his uncle had made sure that his mom maintained her bills. Mickey never thought that his life would change so much when his uncle passed, but it did.

Two months later, times started to get hard. Bills were late, food was scarce, and his mom started to come home later than usual to take on extra shifts. His uncle used to make sure that Mickey's mom didn't work extra shifts. He loved her and called her the best big sister in the entire world. Every time he saw his nephew, he asked him to show him a test grade, interim report, book report—anything, to show that he was doing good in school. And every time, he used to give Mickey money for his pocket. Mickey loved him for that of, course. He had plenty of charisma that everybody wanted and unfortunately, someone took it away.

Walking to school was agonizing because the people in the streets knew his uncle and they knew he was his nephew. They also knew that since his uncle was gone, he was broke.

"Hey little man, you tryna make some extra money?" a tall man asked Mickey. Draco was a street hustler his uncle used to hang with a lot.

"No thanks, I have school," he replied daily, repeatedly.

One day when Mickey came home from school, he tried to turn on his bedroom light. It didn't work and he furiously kept flicking it off and on, off and on, off and on. Nothing. Went into the kitchen and started flicking that light switch. Off and on, off and on, off and on. Nothing. At first, he thought that it was a problem with the lightbulb but soon came to reality when he looked into his mom's room and saw her sitting on the bed, looking defeated with candles lit and tears in her eyes.

When she saw her son, she ran to him and hugged him. "We are going to get through, the Lord will make a way," she said with sad but hopeful eyes.

All he could think was that God was punishing them for no reason. *Why us?* he wondered. His mom was a strong woman just trying to do the right thing and he felt like God was absent that night. For the rest of the night, he sat in the corner of his room thinking, sweating, and crying. The next day when he walked to school, the same thing as usual happened but this time around his answer was different.

"Hey lil' man, you tryna make a lil' money?" Draco asked.

Before Mickey gave him an answer, he looked at his car, his clothes, the jewelry on his neck and wrist, and even the breakfast he was eating. For a second, he closed his eyes and thought about the tears falling from his mother's face the night before.

Mickey took a deep breath and replied, "Yeah."

3
School Days

"**Y**o bro, you want your fruit cup?" Mickey asked. I handed him the fruit cup as we stood in our normal spot in the school's rundown courtyard.

As we ate, I noticed a girl staring at me. "Yo Mickey, what is this girl's problem man? She is staring me down hard," I said, as we made eye contact.

"Go over there and see what she wants, bro," Mickey said as he tilted his head and urged me to go over.

I gave in and started to walk over to her. On the way, I had to pass a lot of ninth graders who still didn't know how to act. "Hey, is your name Joe?" asked one of the kids.

I told him, "Yeah," and walked away. I could hear him still rambling on about how much I looked like his cousin Joe. "Stupid freshmen," I mumbled. As I got closer to the girl, I noticed she was surrounded by a group of friends. I was hoping this would turn out well but most of the time something dumb happened.

"What's up, my name is Deon," I said as I extended my hand.

"Umm, I don't know where your hand been boy, no offense," she fired back.

"Fair enough, so why you keep looking at me?" I asked her, looking nonchalant.

"I don't want nothing, but my friend likes you," she replied.

"Okay, point her out to me and I will see what's up," I said. She pointed across at a girl that was definitely not my type. When her friend noticed she was pointing her out to me, she started talking loudly to the other friend she was eating with.

"So, are you interested in her?" the first girl asked.

I looked over at her friend again and then right back at her. "Sure, I'm interested. I'm about as interested as a healthy vegetarian is interested in buying a chicken shack." They all laughed hysterically. "Look, I don't mean to be mean—no pun intended—but I need someone that don't seem so young acting," I said.

"Oh, so do I seem young acting to you?" she said, hands on her hips.

"Yeah, I'm not going to lie, you do," I said, waiting for her to lash out at me.

"Wow, did y'all hear that? I am *not* young acting," she said with a pouty face.

"Are you a freshman?" I asked.

She blushed and looked at her friends. "So—I'm still not young acting."

I looked her up and down. "Talk is cheap, so prove me wrong," I said. Her friends started to blush. She smiled so hard that I could see practically all of her teeth.

"How do you want me to do that?" she asked.

I smoothly grabbed her hand and gently grasped her phone. I put my number in.

"Why? You can't have my number." she said.

"From what I was hearing, you mature, ain't you? You make that decision and text me when you ready," I said smoothly.

From what I saw, it was working because she was speechless and smiling and blushing with her friends. I walked off, knowing I pulled off something unexpected. The only reason I didn't get her number was because I didn't want to pull out my raggedy-ass flip phone.

As soon as I came pacing back, Mickey smiled and nodded his head. "Yo bro, you got game. I saw all those girls smiling and blushing man," he said.

"So are y'all ready to present your projects or nah?" Janie asked.

"I know I am. Everybody going to be like daaaaaaaaaaaang when they see this amazing project," Jamal replied.

"I got mine too," Mickey said with a smirk. We all gave him a crazy look. "I got this girl to do it for me and she in honor classes," he said, smiling. We all shook our heads and started to laugh.

I put my empty tray on top of the ragged, blue garbage can next to me.

"Hey, can you put this over there too?" Janie said, extending her tray to me.

"Do I look like your butler?" I responded.

"Yep, you sure do. Now put it on the trash can, boy," she said, chuckling. I snatched the tray out of her hand and threw it on the garbage can. "What's your project about anyway?"

I looked the other way and didn't answer. Janie shook her head and stared in the opposite direction. The bell rung and it was now time for English class.

I took out my notebook and wrote something that would relax me.

This will either show my talents or show my fears
No need to worry because when the time is near
You have to make sure that you give it all
* you have*
make them think, make them smile, make
* them cry, make them laugh*

When we walked into English class, the room was already full. We got tons of stares as we paced down the aisle to our seats. We usually sat in the back corner of the classroom because that made it easier to not get blamed for talking. Everybody was busy trying to get their projects together.

"I hope you all have your projects because if it's late, then it's a letter grade off," Ms. Copeland, our English teacher said sternly.

One guy raised his hand. Ms. Copeland pointed to him.

"I got my project on email. Is it okay if I print it out real quick?" he asked.

The look on her face showed her annoyance. "Nope, you can just pull it up on here and present it," she said as she pointed to the computer and overhead.

"Never mind, I just ain't got it today," he said, embarrassed. Everybody in class started laughing, including us.

"Damn, that could've been me, D," Mickey whispered to me.

"Yeah, I know," I said, laughing.

Ms. Copeland sat down. She was my favorite teacher. She had a way of making me like school. She didn't see me as a boy from the hood, but as a kid with potential. I always worked harder for her than any other teacher. "So, Deon, do you want to go first?" she asked. I was now in shock and didn't know what to do because I did not want to go first.

"Man, I wanted to set the tone, Ms. Copeland," Jamal objected.

"Of course, Jamal, come up here and show us what you have," she replied. Jamal got up, not knowing that he'd just saved me from embarrassment.

He pulled out his flash drive and inserted it into the classroom computer that was in the front of the class on the left side. Ms. Copeland sat on the right, and the projector screen was in the middle. The video started and Tupac's song "Changes" started playing. Pictures started to appear. Frederick Douglass,

Harriet Tubman, Martin Luther King Jr., Malcolm X, etc. It was a pretty good project. After the video was over, the whole class started to clap. Jamal put his fist in the air to symbolize black power.

"Great job Jamal, you set the tone and that might be the best one. Let's see who can compete," she said as she stared the class down. After four more projects were presented, Janie raised her hand to go. She got up, carrying a folded-up poster. "What is that Janie?" Ms. Copeland asked.

Janie unfolded her poster. When she turned it around, everyone was in awe. "Wow, Janie, you have some serious talent," Ms. Copeland said. The project was a drawing of Frederick Douglass holding his fist in his hand while holding a book tight, close to his chest. It had to be the best project thus far for the class. "What made you draw this, Janie?" she asked.

"Drawing is something I enjoy and what better way to celebrate it then by giving respect to history?" she replied.

"You getting an A and that was the best one yet," Ms. Copeland said. Jamal started to look disappointed until Janie sat down. She stuck her tongue out at him and he just shook his head.

Mickey raised his hand next. He paced to the front of the class. "I decided to stick to the original plan and do a book report. I know it's not creative but it's a grade," he said. Mickey read off his paper for five minutes. He tripped over so many words that Ms. Copeland asked if it was *his* book report. By the time he finished, half the class was asleep. As the rest of the students continued presenting, I figured I would start practicing to see if I could memorize my poem.

"Deon, you are next on the list," Ms. Copeland announced.

I got up without my paper. My stomach started to develop a knot. It felt as if time was standing still as my heart begin to race. The whole class started to look up and pay attention. "Um, I wrote a poem and I tried to memorize it to the best of my ability so if I mess up, forgive me y'all," I said nervously. *Here we go.*

The first words of the poem ran through my head. *Is it still true... Is it still true...* My heart was about to jump out of my chest from how nervous I was, but I had to do it.

Is it still true?
Is it still true that we are all inherently equal
when Sean Bell taking fifty shots to the
* chest is just another sequel*
to the tragic death of Emmett Till

but still, we constantly bleed out of our
  mental, battling the vicious cycle,
clutching onto every dear word written in our
  precious Bibles,
as words blast off, piercing the soul like rifles
that are shooting down every dream and
  epiphany that's left in me
So, tell me, is it still true that we can be
  whoever we wanna be
in this precious land of the free?
Or are we holding on to the lies cause we need
  something to believe
Is it still true that my father loves me,
though I'm nothing more than a memory in
  his brain,
instead of being a father, he fell in love with
  cocaine,
so who is there to blame? no one.
I just hope he comes around before life's clock
  stops ticking,
and my soul grows cold, and my heart stops
  wishing
So tell me—is it still true that U.S. Africans
  are Americans

when the road we're heading down is just
leading to oppressed again
If not with chains from masters, then
fathers without masters,
As they lower their degrees, getting further
away from sons
by just packing up their lives and preparing to run
So, let us scatter back to a time when all the
skies were once blue,
when the flowers once grew...
and all the answers to these questions were
all once TRUE...

"That's it," I said. I got an uproar of cheers from my classmates.

"Great job, Mr. Sanders, you are amazing at spoken word," Ms. Copeland said.

I smiled and took my seat and waited for the bell to ring. I felt on top of the world. I felt like I could fly if I wanted to. After the final bell, we all met up with each other outside of school.

"Yo, y'all projects was dope but mine was the best," Mickey said.

"Please, everybody almost fell asleep, negro," Janie said, looking annoyed.

"No, forget all that, I know y'all hear my boy Malcolm X with that poetry piece," Jamal replied. Mickey smirked and gave me a playful punch to the shoulder.

"I got to go work with my Uncle Pete at his garage. He got a car he's supposed to be working on and wants me to help, so I will catch up to y'all," Jamal said as he walked off.

We signaled him the peace sign and kept walking. "I got a job too," Mickey said. He pulled out a quarter bag of weed. "Yo bro, if you sell it with me, you be getting paid." he said with a smile. He gave Janie the bag and she held it up to her nose and smelled it.

"This is some strong stuff right here," she said.

"Want some extra money? Then you need to talk to Ricky. He got all the chronic," Mickey said, trying to persuade me.

"Man, I have to get back to you about that," I replied.

"Aight cool, later folks," Mickey said as he went in the other direction.

Janie and I walked in silence for about a minute. "You know D, you are very talented, and you surprised me," she said.

"I appreciate that; you pretty talented your damn self," I replied. I glanced at her and noticed she was blushing.

"Thanks man, I been drawing ever since I was little. I always had dreams of making my own cartoon," she said, smiling while looking up in the air.

"How do you do that?" I asked.

"It's a computer program. My parents bought it for me last Christmas and I'm still learning how to use it."

Smiling, I said, "I didn't know you did stuff like that."

She chuckled. "So is poetry your dream or you trying to be something else?"

I looked up at the clouds and for a quick second, thought about what I wanted to do. I knew I was good at writing poetry but taking it on the road might be a stretch. "I don't really know, to be honest with you," I replied.

"Bro, you might need to start rapping. You already got a good flow with spoken-word, you might as well try. I think you might be dope," she said enthusiastically.

I looked at her, puzzled. She was making sense and I really thought I should try it. "Doesn't sound like a bad plan," I replied. We walked in silence until we reached her street.

"You're going to that teen party that's coming up next week?" she asked.

"Heck yeah, that junk be more live than the prom," I replied excitedly. She smiled and glanced down. Something wet hit my face. "Aww damn, it's about to rain."

Since my place was the closest, we ran there. After we reached my apartment, she asked if she could fix her hair and take off her wet shirt in the bathroom. I told her, "Sure."

I turned on the TV in the front room and flipped through channels. Janie stopped by the couch on the way back from the bathroom when she noticed me staring at her like I was seeing a different person. She took the scarf out of her hair and that was the first time I had ever seen how beautiful she was. I had never seen a girl look so good wearing basketball shorts and a tank top. I wasn't used to seeing her without baggy jeans.

"Dang, what's up with all this?" I said in a squeaky voice.

She laughed. "What you mean man? This my comfortable look," she said.

"Got some butt but you still butt ugly, though," I said with a silly smile.

"Yeah right, you funny," she said with a smirk.

"Naw, forreal though; why you never come to school looking good?" I asked. Her irritation was obvious by the look on her face.

"Oh, just because I don't wear what those other hoodrats wear doesn't mean I'm a bum," she said, smirking and standing with her hands on her hips.

I laughed and decided to let my feelings get involved. "Naw shawty, but forreal, you are a Shaq," I said.

"A *shack?!* Janie exclaimed. "I know this fool is not calling me a small beat-down house," she said, rolling her eyes. I laughed again.

"No, not a shack—I'm talking about the basketball player's shoe. Look, a Jordan is similar to a Shaq. Remember in elementary when half the people in our class wore Shaqs and half wore Jordans? You were popular either way whether you wore a Shaq or Jordan because to us they looked good and everybody wanted them," I said.

She just stared at me. "So, what's your point?" she asked.

"They all look the same. People just put a fictitious value on it," I said.

"So, a Jordan has a higher value than a Shaq, though," she said.

"Hmm you right, but Jordans and Shaqs probably have the same expiration date on them—it depends on how you take care of them. Even though something is expensive doesn't mean it has a higher value, Janie. Water is the most precious thing on this earth and for the most part, it doesn't cost us a dime to even touch it."

"Well, can I be water then because your logic is confusing me. 'Water is the most precious thing on this earth and doesn't cost us a dime,'" she repeated sarcastically.

"Whatever, you can be water. Who gives a damn?" I said with a laugh. I switched to an action movie. After watching it in silence for five minutes, she spoke up again.

"So, what's up wit' yo lil girlfriend?" she asked.

"Shoot, you tell me," I said as I changed the channel.

"You like those ratchet ass girls?" she said, laughing.

"So, ain't nothin' wrong wit' a little bit of thug in ya," I said as I went into the kitchen to get some chips for us.

"What kind of guys do you think would be interested in me?" Janie asked.

The question caught me so off guard that my heart dropped a little. I couldn't believe she'd asked me for dating advice.

"What you mean, like hookin' up?" I asked, wide-eyed.

"Yeah, because I'm kind of interested in a boyfriend. Never had no true one," she said, her cheeks turning red.

In my mind, I didn't believe that. "I don't know... you pretty straight forward; maybe you just need somebody real," I said as I handed her a bag of chips.

"Thanks, and you might be right," she replied.

I get two cans of soda out of the fridge and handed one to her. "Didn't you hear what I say about Jordans and Shaqs? Plenty of people are looking for a Shaq; matter of fact, we can find somebody at the party for you," I replied.

She looked at me weird. "I don't know if somebody at a party is genuine enough."

I take a sip of my soda and set it on the small table next to the couch. "Can't knock it until you try it," I said.

"Yeah, yeah. I gotta go, you think you can walk me home?" she asked.

"Nah, my legs hurt," I said.

She sucked on her teeth and headed to the door.

"Yo I'm just playin', stop being so sensitive!" I yelled, grabbing her shirt and jeans off the couch.

"Thanks," she replied as we headed out the door.

As we get on the main street, I told her about my situation with the freshman girl.

"Hey, call her and talk to her. If she feelin' you, she will agree to go to the party with you," she said, playing with and clicking her long fingernails. We walked in silence until we arrived at her house. "I'll see you tomorrow, big dawg," she said, giving me a fist bump.

"Aight homie," I answered. She walked to her door and turned around.

"Yo maybe we can do like that art and poetry thing together one day," she said, excitedly.

"That will be dope, hit me up on the cell and we can talk about it when you ready," I said.

"Cool. I'll see ya," she said, as she waved and went inside.

For the first time, I felt like I'd really gotten to know Janie personally. I kind of liked her but I had always looked at her as one of the homies. I hoped she found a dude that would respect her.

I couldn't walk home in silence by myself, so I took out my phone and called Keisha, the freshman girl I'd met in the courtyard at school. "You wanna go to that party this Friday?"

She laughed and said, "Maybe," in a flirty voice.

I laughed, paused, then said with confidence, "See you Friday." We both laughed, said our goodbyes, and hung up.

•••

Friday, I woke up and went through my normal routine. At six, I started walking to the spot. I was wearing something casual for school because I planned on borrowing an outfit from my cousin before the party. When I arrived at the spot, everybody else was already there laughing and talking.

"What up bro, take a swig of this right here," Mickey said, and gave me an airplane bottle of liquor.

I put it in my bookbag. "I will probably drink it when I hit that party up tonight. Appreciate it bro," I said, giving him a fist bump.

"So D, I've been thinking about that art project and I was thinking maybe we could do it tomorrow evening," Janie said.

"What art project y'all talkin' about?" interrupted Jamal.

"It's this art and poetry thing, it's no big deal," I said to Jamal. "Yeah, that's cool," I replied to Janie.

Mickey looked at me and Janie with an obnoxious look. "Man, y'all betta set y'all nerd asses down somewhere, talkin' about some art and poetry," he said, chuckling.

"Stop hating, Mickey," Janie said, with an expression that said she wasn't playing.

"I mean, you ain't even that good though. You're definitely not good enough for 'da man' to offer you a job," he said, laughing.

"Yo, that shit ain't funny, Mickey. To keep it a hunnit, it seems like you're hating because we doing something positive with our talent," I said seriously.

"Oh, and I don't have any?" he replied. "Y'all think y'all special because you can do poetry and you can do artwork? Man, get outta here bruh. I already told y'all where the real money is and maybe if y'all stop cappin' with your drawing pads and diaries, we could make a lil' money, forreal."

I shook my head and sat down on a brown, abandoned, rusty table that looked like it had been left by someone who never cared to come back for it.

"Come on now. I gave all y'all bottles today and I got myself a big one, and only been working for two days! Now that's money, and that's how you go out and get it," Mickey said ecstatically like he just gave a motivational speech.

I looked closer at Mickey and noticed his eyes were bloodshot. He was drunk. As soon as I realized it, Janie and Jamal did too. They looked as worried as me.

"Like bruh, bruh, you need to put the bottle down bruh, we ain't even at the party yet," I said.

"Man we ain't even in school yet," Jamal said, shaking his head.

"Nobody drunk. I'm high though and a little tipsy," Mickey said, putting the bottle back in his bookbag.

"So, you meant what you said?" Janie asked Mickey.

"Yeah I did, because we live in a white society and nobody gets to do things like that," Mickey replied.

I looked at him, shaking my head. "Bruh, you wrong, it ain't no such thing as a white society." I looked at Jamal and Janie for their approval.

"I mean we do kinda live in a white society D, that ain't no secret," Jamal said.

Janie sighed. "Yeah I ain't gonna lie, we do," she said, crossing her arms on her chest.

"See bruh, we do," Mickey said.

I looked at each of them in disappointment. "See, thinking like that, how are we going to see progress? Y'all steady screamin' out we live in a white society, yet we had a black president. You don't have the right to discourage what we gifted at, bruh. Selling drugs or being an athlete is not the only way to make it out of the hood, bro. There are other ways we can do that. You can sell drugs bruh, but that ain't me," I said.

"Yo momma struggles and is poor just like mine. This is the only way to help our mommas. D, writing poetry is cool, but you ain't got no money like this," he said, opening his bookbag to show me.

"Whatever." I walked towards the school.

"Don't be salty bruh, are we cool?" Mickey asked, running up to me and extending his fist. "I'm just sayin' that you can make a little money dawg, I ain't been tryin to stunt on your dreams or nothin' man. I just see a good opportunity for us to make some money and I wanted us to make it together, that's all," he said.

I looked at him for a minute and gave him the fist bump.

"I gotcha bro, we're cool," I answered as we walked to school.

At lunchtime, Mickey hooked us up with some honey mustard wings as his way to apologize for the comments he'd said to Janie and me. "Yo, ain't you supposed to talk to shorty over there?"

I almost forgot about my girl! I looked over and saw Keisha sneaking looks at me while she was talking to her friends. I made my way over there. Her friends slowly started to move out of the spotlight as I walked towards them. She smiled at me hard and gave me a big hug.

"So what time are you picking' me up tonight?" she asked.

Was she serious? "I thought we were going to meet each other there because I'm rockin' with my friends for a minute," I said, trying to hide the fact I didn't have a car.

"You can't come pick me up afta you hang wit' em?" she asked, popping her gum.

"Well, umm, I don't have a car, baby," I said, embarrassed.

"Well, I guess I'll see you out there," she said.

I gave her a hug, but she didn't hug me back. As soon as I walked away from her, I could see her friends laughing in my direction. I hoped she wasn't trying to play me.

"Let me guess. She trippin' over a car, huh?" Mickey asked.

"Yeah man, she acts like she can't just meet me out there," I said.

"That's how those freshman girls are, bruh. Don't be looking forward to seeing her at the party either. She's probably going to be there with someone else," Mickey said.

After we ate and talked about nothing for the next ten minutes, we all headed to English class.

"Somebody explain to me what Hamlet means when he says, 'To be or not to be,'" Ms. Copeland instructed the class.

Dave, the smartass of the class, raised his hand. She pointed to him.

"He was questioning if he should be the killer or not to avenge the tragic death of his royal father," Dave said with supreme arrogance and confidence.

"Not quite Dave, but you are sort of on the right track though," the teacher replied.

Dave displayed an astonished defeated look which I enjoyed because the dude thought he knew everything.

"How about you, Deon? You're good at poetry, this should be right up your alley," she said with a smile.

Lucky for me, I'd read the play and knew what she was talking about. Usually, I never read homework assignments but ever since the day I read poetry in class, I was feeling sort of different about learning.

"I think he's trying to make a correlation between staying alive and committing suicide," I answered.

"Perfect answer, that's the exact meaning," she said, smiling.

Everyone in class started to look at me like I stole something. I shrugged my shoulders slightly.

"Ha, I see you getting those cool points with Ms. Copeland bruh, I ain't mad atcha," Mickey whispered from across the table.

"You already know, bruh, she's gonna be mine soon," I said, as we both laughed quietly.

Janie gave me a thumbs up. Jamal was asleep. Mickey slapped him on the back of the neck to wake him up.

"Yo man, y'all play too much," Jamal said. We all laughed quietly.

"Okay, I want you to all write a page about what you think about Hamlet in Act Three. You have twenty minutes," Ms. Copeland said.

Since I knew the story, it only took me seven minutes to write the page; so, I had some time left to write some poetry. I was good at poetry, but I also loved hip hop music. I mean, I was a HUGE fan of hip hop. Maybe that was something I should express.

A Fan of Hip-Hop...?
Allow me to reintroduce myself,
My name is Deon and I'm a fan of hip hop
The real hip hop, you know back when it was
  about lyrics stimulating the brain
Like heroine shot off, injected in ya veins
or giving vision to a blind man who the doctor
  said would never ever see again
So, who is there to blame for the gunshots at
  night?
The rappers or trappers—but the trappers
  wanna be rappers, so I guess you can say
  they're synonymous

While the gunshots that're shooting down the dreams and ambitions of the children remain anonymous

So, what do I do?

I try to reverse their psychology by using reverse psychology

dividing the mind like dichotomy

Into a good side and a bad side and putting them both together,

making a whole side of intellectual thoughts

serving as a bulletproof vest for all the shots that hip hop is blasting off

see but not all hip hop is bad, because in a time of DaBaby and Gucci Mane—

who portray an image that violence and crack is the way—

we have the J. Coles, the Kanyes, the Drakes and Jays

who say that pursuing an education and intelligence is always okay

Cause even as a dropout, Kanye went on to late registration, then to graduation,

promoting a message about the power of education

See, most rappers of today are stuck in the
  mentality of N.W.A.
but what they fail to realize is that N.W.A.
  was simply trying to relay a message that
  society didn't wanna hear
not set a trend of murders and dealings up to
  the current year
hip hop used to inspire and heal us, but now
  it's just a bruise
Nas said hip hop is dead while I'll just say its
  confused.

•••

After the bell rang, the teacher told me to come to her desk.

"Deon, the other day when you displayed that wonderful, articulate piece of poetry, I had an idea to enter you into the Young Writers state competition," she said, smiling and putting her hands together.

"What is that?" I asked. She handed me a sheet of paper.

"It's a workshop where great poets, readers, and young artists compete for a scholarship to an art school of their choice," she replied.

I skimmed through the paper. "On here it says that it could be a collaboration thing also?"

"Yes. If you want a partner, tell him or her to sign up through me. They can be another poet, storyteller or artist who can draw on the spot."

I immediately started thinking about Janie. "I'll think about it," I told her, folding up the paper and put it in my pocket.

After school, my friends and I walked to the spot. We were so hyped about tonight.

"Okay homies, this is what we're gonna do. We're going to all go to our cribs first, freshen up, and I'm going to borrow my momma's car and pick you up around nine," Mickey said.

"Alright y'all, I got to go, mom's getting ready for work and she wants to holla at me before she leaves," I said.

Everyone said, "Cool," as I walked off.

"Mom, I'm home!" I yelled as I walked in the apartment.

"Food is on the stove, and how was your day?" she yelled from the back room.

"It was okay. Listen Mom, I was just wondering if we still cool about that party tonight. I can still go, right?" I asked.

"Well, you did everything you suppose to do around here so yeah, sure, and plus I have a night shift so you probably was going to try to sneak out anyway," she answered.

I sat down on the couch with my plate and watched TV. A few hours later, my mom was ready to go.

"What time are you leaving?" she asked as she put on her blue factory jacket.

"Mickey's supposed to be picking me up any minute now," I said as I put on some deodorant.

"Have fun and remember, if I come home before you, it's gonna be a problem, okay?" My mom said with a stern look.

"Yes ma'am, I gotcha," I said and gave her a hug.

"Alright, see ya and remember to put the food up before you go," she said as she walked out.

•••

I checked my phone and saw that it was 8:15. In the bathroom mirror, I profiled to make sure everything was good. I poured a half glass of orange juice and added the shot of liquor that Mickey had given me. I wanted to feel more relaxed and included so I drank it as fast as I could—I didn't feel anything. I put the food in the refrigerator and sat down to watch TV until Mickey knocked on the door. Grabbing my key, I walked to the door and opened it.

Mickey stood there smiling at me. That was no ordinary smile. He obviously had something to say. "Why in the hell are you smiling so dang hard, Mickey?" I asked. I locked the door and closed it behind me. "And where are Jamal and Janie?"

"They're in the car and BRUUUUHHH! JANIE LOOKIN' GOOOOOOOD, " Mickey said with an exaggerated smile, raising his eyebrows and opening his eyes wide.

"What does she have on?" I asked, curious.

"Wait bruh, you'll see. You're going to be like DAAAAAANGGG! Watch," he said, laughing.

We walked down the steps and to his car which was parked directly beside the apartments. Jamal was already in the front and Janie was in the back. I opened the back door and didn't see Janie at first because I was focusing on Jamal's handshake. Then I looked at her and saw that Mickey was right. She had on a little makeup, but just enough to show her beauty. She was wearing a beautiful, skinny, black and white dress that showed off her legs and curves. The best part about it was that it wasn't too revealing or ratchet. It was sexy and classy—just like Janie.

"Guess what?" she said to me.

"What's up?" I replied.

"I'm about to quit smoking, D," she said with a smile.

"I don't think that possible, cuz tonight you on FIYYAAA!" Mickey said, laughing.

"BOOOOO! You a cornball for that one, bruh," said Jamal, also laughing.

"That's wassup. I support cha doin' yo thang, that's a pretty big step," I said, giving her a fist bump. Mickey stopped at a red light.

"Man D! Shut yo ass up. You act like she pill-popping or something, talkin' bout 'that's a big step,'" Mickey said, chuckling. Jamal joined in with a laugh.

"Thanks, D!" Janie said loudly, making sure that Mickey and Jamal knew that my comment was insightful.

We rode without talking for a few minutes until Janie broke the silence. "Guess what Mickey, I told D that I liked you," she said.

"Oh really—so D hiding stuff from me now, huh? Good timin' though because you looking bad tonight," Mickey said, laughing. I looked at her, chuckling.

"I was just playing though, with your peanut head," she said, smiling. Everyone laughed at that, including Mickey.

"I don't give a damn anyway, you like a lil' sista to me and that would definitely be insect," Mickey said.

"It's called *incest*, dummy. Insect is a damn bug," said Jamal, shaking his head as Janie and I burst into laughter.

We pulled up to the club and it was packed. "Aight y'all, this is how we're going to do it," said Mickey, as he pulled out a bottle and four shot glasses. "We all going to take two shots and get lit in there." He passed out the shot glasses.

After we guzzled down the shots, we were ready to go in. At least thirteen people were in front of us, waiting to get into the club. A big, black, muscular security guard with a deep scar on his right cheek was at the door checking each person for weapons. "Damn, it's live in here already, bruh," Mickey said, rubbing his hands together.

"You think yo girl in here, D?" Jamal asked as we moved up in line.

"She ain't text me yet so I don't know," I replied. I checked my phone and still, there were no new messages from Keisha. Finally, it was our turn to be checked.

"You're good," the security guard said as he pointed to Janie to go in. "Turn around and spread out your arms," he said to me. After checking me, he said, "You're good."

I walked in and saw Janie standing by the register to pay. The cashier was fine and looked to be in her mid-twenties. I scanned the club scene and it was crazy. At first glance, I saw people on the dance floor, fine girls, and a great atmosphere. Mickey and Jamal walked in and went to the register to pay. "Ten dollars," said the cashier. We all paid her ten then she put green wristbands on our arms, one by one.

"Man, I'm about to get all the numbers in here, bruh; all these girls gonna be all over me," Mickey said as we walked in. We found a table and sat down to scope the club out. "YO, YO GIRL RIGHT THERE, BRUH—YOU SEE HER?" Mickey yelled out as he pointed to my potential girlfriend.

I got up and made my way through the crowd to her. Keisha was sitting at a table with a group of friends—one other girl and three guys. When I reached the table, her expression changed to one of disappointment. I crouched down. "Wassup girl," I said.

"Hey," she replied.

"Why you ain't text me?" I asked.

"I dunno," she responded as she joined her friends' conversation.

It was starting to feel tense and I had the feeling I wasn't wanted. "Is everything good between us?" I asked.

"Look, clearly she doesn't want your broke, no-car ass, so you can leave," one of her girlfriends said.

"Shut up girl, this ain't got nothin' to do wit' you," I said, losing my temper.

One of the guys got up and started talking trash. At this point, I blocked everything out because I felt like she was playing me just as Mickey had predicted in school. When the bouncer with the scar showed up, he grabbed me and led me out of the club. As soon as we passed by Mickey, he and the crew were right behind me.

"What'd I do?" I asked the bouncer as we exited the doors of the club. Mickey and the crew followed us out of the club and waited on the bouncer's response.

"Look, no fighting is going to be taking place in this club and if you want to get back in, you have to tell me what happened. If I don't like it, you have to take yo ass home, are we clear?!" the bouncer said, as we stared face to face.

I looked at Mickey, Janie, and Jamal then took a deep breath because I had to tell the bouncer how I got played. "Aight man, this what happened. My girl—well, she was sort of my girl—basically we was supposed to be kickin' it together tonight at the party and when I tried to talk to her, her and her bit- I mean friends started trippin' over nothin'. Then that's when ol' boy tried to get tough on me for no reason and I don't even know him. Sir, I'm just tryna have a good time with my friends, I'm not tryin' to start no altercations in yo spot, trust me on that," I said as I held my hands up sincerely.

He looked at me with a serious, ugly look. "Okay, you can go back in, but if I see you over there again, you outta here. You understand?" he said.

Looking away, I said, "Yes, I understand."

Janie looked at me angrily. "Don't let those girls and those fakes ruin our night," she said.

"Yeah bruh, forget them. I ain't tryna fight tonight," Mickey said, putting his hands up.

"From now on, forget them, let's party!" Jamal added, as we walked back in the club.

Everybody in the club was now on the dance floor. A couple of girls were dancing and waiting for a dude to approach them. Mickey approached one of the girls slowly as all of the guys just sat and watched, waiting for something to happen. He approached her and she turned around and accepted his invitation to dance with her. She moved her body effortlessly to the beat of the music. Mickey grabbed her waist and followed her movements and for a moment, those two were the life of the party.

"D! You see the homie gettin' it in, hahahaha," Jamal said, pointing and laughing.

I took a look at Janie and saw she was sitting with her legs crossed, smiling. Her amicable attitude filled the room. The atmosphere there was exactly what I needed to calm my nerves. I walk up behind one of the girls and grabbed her waist. She nonchalantly turned around to see what I looked like. She winked at me, casually giving me the signs to dance. I moved in closer and she started to grind on me. Out of the corner of my eye, I noticed Janie watching me. She half smiled but also looked somewhat disappointed. After our three-minute dance, I made my way back to where Janie was sitting.

"What's up wit you?" I asked her.

"Just don't feel like dancing," she said, shrugging.

I grabbed her hand and pulled her gently to the dance floor. "You see all these guys? They're all looking for a dance," I said, pointing toward a group of guys who were just standing around, hoping to get lucky.

"I don't want to dance with those fools. What do you think I am—desperate?" she said, with a tired look on her face.

"You have to open yourself up, Janie, or nobody is going to approach you. What you need is a dummy test," I said, watching one of the other girls dancing.

Janie slapped my shoulder to regain my attention. "What do you mean about a dummy test?" she asked.

"Dance with one of these dudes to get the attention of the others," I said as I started to walk away to go dance with another girl.

She stopped me. "How about *you* be the dummy? You already dancing with somebody so that should draw attention for the both of us."

I was about to say no but then thought, *why not?* She turned around and started moving her hips gracefully while I grabbed her by the waist. The energy that we felt was so refreshing and the comfort level was beyond words. We danced the whole song through and—to tell you the truth—I wanted to dance again. After the dance, I sat down and watched everybody else dance, including her. Some guys talked while dancing with her, trying to persuade her to take their number or Snapchat info. Some succeeded, some failed. Watching my friends having fun was okay but I was unhappy sitting there. Yes, this was a social spot but at the same time, it was just full of attention seekers. I ain't really with that. In fact, I was about ready to go home.

As soon as I was about to tell my friends I was ready, people started to scream and run for the exit. Gunshots rang out. After rushing out of the club to the car, I waited for my friends, hoping they were good. On cue, all of them ran out at the same time, laughing and telling me to get in the car so we could leave.

"Man, that was crazy, people are really shootin' out here," said Mickey.

We all laughed but a part of me was still traumatized. Why did we do that? Act like it was all cool when really, we were scared. Mickey stopped by Carlitos, an all-night burger joint. They had the best burgers. Since none of the homies had any money, Mickey blessed us by offering to buy us all No. 1 meals.

"Yo, get the special sauce, it is bomb yo!" yelled Jamal.

"What you know about that, youngin'," asked Mickey, turning around to look at Jamal.

"I know all about that bro, I'm the best when it comes to flavor," Jamal said.

Mickey and I burst into laughter and Janie just kept a straight face.

"He's forreal though; my brother is a great cook," she said. We stopped laughing and stared at her in disbelief.

"How you know how to cook, Jamal, and why didn't we know this?" I asked.

"The same reason why you hid your poetry from us—you didn't want to look like a clown or nerd," he said, disappointedly.

Mickey parked the car at the spot and while we ate, Jamal started telling us the story about how he first started cooking. Turned out his mom did a little catering on the side for family and close friends. She had dreams of being a chef at one point in her life but had to abandon those dreams when she had a family. At seven years old, Jamal used to come home from school and his mom would cook cheap budget gourmet meals so Jamal became interested in all of it. He knew her secret recipes and even had his own. He knew how to cook, bake, and grill. He even cooked when she was at work and Janie could validate that his meals were bomb.

And to think I thought this fool was big for no reason. What made me really mad though was that we could have been eating great gourmet meals for lunch.

When we were finished, it was almost one o'clock and we all decided to get home because we knew the shooting was going to be reported on the news the next day. Or even worse, the word was around the streets and we all decided before all of that happened, it would be a good idea if our parents saw us first.

When I got dropped off, I told all my friends, "Bye," and hurried past the drug addicts and winos surrounding my project building. I went straight into my room and got out my notebook. Writing was definitely on my mind tonight. Sometimes that was my only escape.

HOW CAN YOU JUDGE ME
How can you judge me without knowing the
   person that's within
How can you categorize me by the color of my skin
Why would you degrade me, how could you tell
   those lies

Why do you envy me because of the color of my eyes
What's wrong with me? Why am I the scum
  of the earth
And why does it seem as if I have been cursed
  since birth
What do I have to do so that I can be
  treated like a human
Why do you judge me by how I look rather
  than what I'm doing
You judge me out of the womb; you hated me
  out of the uterus
I was still a child, life—I was new to it.
Yet you judge me, you even took me from my land,
said to me over and over, I would never be a man
But we still rose as a people, walking hand
  and hand,
finishing with the words of Barack Obama
  saying, YES WE CAN!

The next morning, my mom woke me up to discuss what happened in the club. As we'd guessed, word of mouth traveled fast.

"I would tell you not to go to any more parties and things, but you aren't the problem, ignorance is," my mom said to me. She was right.

My hood was the type of place where I would be shielded but I could still be at risk of getting hurt. At least I felt protected by the people in my hood: drug addicts, dealers, whatever else you could imagine. I've known them for years and developed a relationship with them. I knew when people thought of my neighborhood, they only saw pimps, addicts, and thugs. As for me, I saw people I've known my entire life. People that were systematically trapped in an environment that I was determined to make it out of.

4

Saturday's Tragedy

Saturday afternoon I was about to meet my friends at the spot. I had nothing better to do, plus I decided to join the poetry contest. But I also wanted to ask Janie if she would be willing to be my partner for the contest. She was a great artist and I wanted her to showcase her art just as I wanted to showcase my poetry.

As I walked downstairs, I saw a couple of people in Ricky's crew, Malcolm and Dorsett, and they looked upset. They were a couple of the top guys in the crew. Some people referred to them as "cray cray" because they were crazy as hell. They seemed to be arguing about something and I knew it had to be serious because they had white tank tops on and every time somebody from the crew wore a white tank top, something was going down. I partially overheard the argument and it sounded like somebody from their crew had gotten robbed. I didn't like the sound of that because that meant violence will ensue all over the city.

I start walking to the spot. As I walked, I started to think about my future. Sometimes, as young men we didn't stop to think about what was ahead of us and how much life we actually had not lived yet. A lot of kids were like, "I'm lucky if I make it to eighteen." It was sad because that was only about a fourth of a person's life expectancy. I didn't know about anyone else, but I wanted to make it past eighteen. I wanted to live the dream.

What was the dream? I didn't know yet. I got to the spot and saw all of my friends there. Everyone was wearing basketball shorts and a shirt, including Janie. Ever since I'd seen her at the club, I looked at her differently. She shouldn't be dressed like us, or maybe I was trippin'. Mickey had his Bluetooth speaker and was listening to DaBaby. "Maaaaan, Baby go hard," he said, while rapping the song.

We laughed in agreement as we nodded to DaBaby's song, "Suge." Janie and I made eye contact and I came to the conclusion that I should talk to her about the poetry contest.

"Can I speak to you over here, real quick?" I said, pointing to a place with more privacy.

She said, "Yeah," and followed me.

I clasped my hands together and I didn't know why but I was nervous about asking her this question.

Maybe it was because this was the first time I'd ever asked a friend to do something outside of what we usually did.

"Well, you know I do poetry, right?" I said.

"Duh, Deon," she said sarcastically.

"Yeah, you right, that was a stupid question. Umm, there's this poetry contest coming up for the school and it's for a pretty good prize and I just wondered if you wanted to maybe-"

"Yeah Deon," she interrupted. "I would love to collaborate with you. We were supposed to do that anyway."

"Yeah, I know. Just didn't know how you would take it, I guess," I said, scratching my head.

She looked at me and smiled and walked back to the crew.

"What y'all got goin on?" Mickey asked.

"None of your business," I responded as I pulled four Arizona cans out my bookbag.

"Looks good, bro," Mickey said as he took one.

"Well, if you want to know, me and Deon are going to enter the poetry contest together," Janie said, glancing at me.

"Dang, what's next? A room?" Mickey said while Jamal laughed.

"Yeah, whatever, just know that me and her are winning this thing." I put my arm around Janie in a friendly manner.

"Well, I hope you guys win because they gonna have prizes for the winners and Janie don't go nowhere without me, so I know I'll be benefitting from that," said Jamal.

"What you talkin' about, big head—I don't go everywhere with you," Janie said.

We all looked around with unconvinced expressions as Janie rolled her eyes at us and sipped her Arizona. Today was a beautiful sunny day, one of those cookout and barbeque days. Maybe we needed to go find one and say, "What's up cousins," just to get a plate.

As we drank our Arizonas, a gray Honda Civic slowly pulled up to us. We didn't know if we should run or just see what's up. The car was now ten feet away from us. I was nervous because I'd heard about things like this but didn't know what was going to happen. I knew Mickey had a gun hidden by the pile of junk that surrounded us. I was terrified. By the time I reached to grab the gun, the window rolled down and only thing I heard the mystery guy say was, "Ay Mickey. What's good, homie?"

Mickey shook his head, grinning. "What up Don? Imma be on the block later, cuzzo," he replied. "That's my cousin, y'all," he said to us. To Don, he said, "Matter of fact, I was about to go re-up and get these bags together."

"Come by the bando," said Don. "You can bring your friends if you want to. We got 2K, pizza, and wings."

Mickey nodded his head and his cousin drove off. He turned to ask us if we wanted to come to the traphouse.

"Man, *hell* no," said Jamal.

Janie followed that up with, "I agree, I'm going home."

Mickey looked at me expectantly. I know I shouldn't go but 2K, pizza, and wings sounded good. "Come on bro, only going to be there for an hour, I promise. You can eat pizza, play a couple of games and boom—we out," he said persuasively.

"Alright bro, but just for an hour bro. You know how I don't like being around stuff like that."

"I gotcha, bro," he said.

We went left as Janie and Jamal went right. I looked back and saw Janie glancing back too. She had a concerned look on her face as if something bad might happen. I had a similar feeling as well.

The traphouse was on Walton Street which was in one of the most dangerous neighborhoods in the city. My apartment complex was like Bel Air compared to Walton Street. When we arrived in the neighborhood, kids were playing outside, drug addicts were walking around like zombies, and drug dealers were posted all around. This was the part of the neighborhood that police didn't pull up to. My momma had said that Walton Street was the result of decades of redlining, and discriminatory housing practices against black people. The house we were about to walk into, commonly referred to as the bando, was actually owned by Ricky. He had a few around the city. This one was full of his best workers.

When we stepped in, five guys were there laughing and talking. Two were handling money, one was sitting on the couch eating pizza and the other two were playing 2K.

"What up, Mickey," everyone said.

"About to get to this paper, y'all already know. This my boy, Deon. He cool as hell and don't start nothing," Mickey said.

"If lil' homie cool wit you, he cool wit us bro," said a guy smoking on the couch.

"Help yo'self to pizza and wings," said Mickey's cousin, one of the two guys counting stacks of money.

I went over and fixed me a plate. Even though the outside of the traphouse looked bad, the inside was pretty well kept up. A nice rug that looked like it could be Persian was spread on the floor. A clean wooden table stood in the middle, and the entertainment system was state-of-the-art. The kitchen had two glass tables. For a traphouse, it was pretty neat. Hell, I would live here. This was one of the trap spots where the best workers were so I could see why it looked that way.

I went and sat beside the guy on the couch. He was knocked out sleeping. I really wanted to drop a sock in his mouth. The two guys playing NBA 2K were into it intensely, yelling at each other. It was the third quarter and I felt that Mickey would probably be done before I could play because he seemed to be working pretty fast. So, I decided to just relax and indulge in my pizza and wings. Mickey and his cousin started talking about the same topic that I'd heard earlier—the robbery. Turned out, Ricky's people had been victims of a string of robberies in the past couple of days. All of them were petty robberies, nothing extreme or involving their best workers. Nobody would dare come here. This place was basically like a secondary headquarters. Anyone would have to be ready for war if they come up in here with some mess.

I was on my second slice of pizza when I heard a knock at the door.

"Who dat?" Mickey said.

I shrugged my shoulders and the guys that were playing 2K immediately stopped the game. They both looked through a crack in the window blinds.

"Aww man, it's Lou!" one of them said. Lou was a tall, charismatic white guy. Everyone knew he was one of their best customers. So they didn't treat him like every other addict but actually had a little respect for him; or at least for his money.

"Ay lil bro, come over here and give this to him," Mickey's cousin said, pointing to me.

"Naw bro, he ain't with none of that. I told you that," Mickey told his cousin.

The dude that had been asleep the whole time suddenly woke up and said, "I'll take that money." He put on his shoes and walked outside. Everybody went back to what they were doing. The game was about over and now the clear-cut winner became obvious. He had a double-digit lead and the guy who was trailing was just putting up threes in the final minute.

"Almost done, D. My house is on the other side so you know you can get this work on 2K after this," he said, lifting his bookbag full of drugs.

As I stood up to get more pizza and wings, the door swung open and one of Mickey's friends was tossed on the floor. Two guys with guns came in and told us, "Nobody move, or we'll shoot!" These guys were tall, muscular, and wearing black ski masks. A few guns lay on the table near the guys who were playing 2K. I hoped they wouldn't be bold enough to try and grab them, but unfortunately, I was wrong.

They reached for their guns as Mickey screamed, "Nooo!" But it was too late. They were shot instantly.

I panicked and ran for the back door. Mickey was right with me. A couple of shots flew by our heads but thank God they missed us. Mickey and I managed to run towards the back of the house while Mickey's cousin, Don, failed to get up. We didn't know if he'd gotten shot or not and just kept running as gunshots blasted through the air. I knew Mickey wanted to turn back and check on his cousin, but at that moment all we could do was run. "C'mon Don!!" Mickey screamed as we bolted towards the door.

"We gotta get to your house," I said to Mickey.

"Come on, Deon!" Mickey yelled at me while going out the back door. I followed him but I could still hear people chasing us. A fence was between the backyard and the neighbor's house. Good thing no cars were in the yard and it seemed like nobody was home. We cut across their yard to get back on the main road.

We seemed to be in the clear and were just down the street from Mickey's house. Pow! Mickey screamed and fell down. The shooter was running towards us and I had to choose whether to just keep going or go back to help Mickey. I decided to go back. We had been friends for too long to turn my back on him. I shielded Mickey from the gunman.

"Get outta here bro, before you die too," Mickey said softly.

"Well, I guess we both are going to have to die because I'm not leaving you," I replied.

I thought the gunman was still after us but all I heard was silence. He was either taking a shortcut, hiding, or running back to join his accomplices. Relieved that Mickey and I were alive, I saw that Mickey had been shot in the back. This was the first time I'd ever seen him cry.

"Take me to the hospital D, take me to the hospital," he said, his voice raspy from the crying.

I helped him up and carried and dragged him to his car. While helping him into the back seat, I told him it was going to be alright. Some people who'd gotten shot tried to act tough which was what I thought Mickey would have done—act like it hadn't phased him. Didn't know he was going to react like that. Sometimes I forgot that we were still kids. So many things had happened within the last week, I felt like our childhood was escaping us. If Mickey made it, maybe this would change his life.

After we drove off, I turned around to see he was bleeding all over the place. Good thing the hospital was about five minutes away. It only took me about two to get there because I was speeding. I didn't want to go *too* fast because the police would have stopped us and there was zero percent chance I would have been able to get out of *that* situation.

I kept looking back every thirty seconds, saying, "Breathe bro, just take it easy and breathe. You're gonna be fine." When we got to the hospital, I parked by the emergency room. I got out of the car, frantic, and the hospital staff member outside figured out what was going on and went for help. Two more came out and lifted Mickey out the car and safely onto a gurney. I followed them into the hospital, telling Mickey that he was going to be alright.

As soon as we neared the operating room, the doctor stopped me. "Sorry kid, but we have to perform surgery. Please try to get in touch with his family if you can," he said as he went through the door.

With trembling hands, I took out my phone and called my mom. She was the only person that could get in touch with Mickey's mom because they worked at the same place and were friends. The phone rang twice then my mom answered.

"Mom, I... I..."

"What's the matter, Deon?"

"I need you to... to get in touch with Mickey's mom and tell her to go to the hospital."

"Oh Lord! What happened? AND WHERE ARE YOU?!"

The tears started to fall now. It really started to hit me that my best friend had just been shot and I'd almost been shot too. "I'm at the hospital... Mickey got shot, Mom, and I was there... I was there," I said, crying uncontrollably.

"Okay, I am on the way now!" Mom yelled and hung up. This was possibly the worst day of my life.

When Mom and Ms. Brown arrived at the hospital, they were both in tears. "What happened, Deon?" Ms. Brown asked.

It was hard to reply because we'd been at the bando. I knew there had been a lot of drugs in there. I knew the bookbag that was in Mickey's car was full of drugs. I knew that I had to tell the truth. Yet, a part of me wanted to hold back, so I did.

"We were at his cousin's house; I forget his name but we were there playing a game and eating pizza and wings and somebody came in and tried to rob his cousin," I said, swallowing a mouthful of tears and spit to keep going. "But it was more of an ambush because they just started shooting and then me and Mickey got away, but somebody shot five times from a distance and two ended up hitting him and..." I couldn't finish and started crying hard. They both hugged me and told me it was going to be okay. I hoped they were right.

5

Friendship

Monday morning, I wasn't ready to go to school yet. I was thankful that at least Mickey didn't die, though. He was in the hospital recovering and I only heard updates from my mom. I got up sluggishly, dragging myself to the bathroom. I didn't even feel like taking a shower. But I thought maybe I should at least wash my face. I knew my friends were going to want to meet me at the spot, but I was going to skip it. I wasn't mad at them or anything, I just didn't need the sorrow. I decided to take a shower so I could meditate and clear my mind a little. After the shower, I brushed my teeth and headed to school.

I went straight to class. School wasn't the same knowing that Mickey was in the hospital. I felt like I was on the verge of losing my best friend not only physically but mentally. I knew that he wasn't going to be the same after this. He'll either be vengeful or end up making peace with the situation. I prayed that he chose peace. After my second block, it was time for lunch. Janie, Jamal, and Mickey were in my third block so I knew I would run into Janie and Jamal at lunch. As soon as I entered the cafeteria, there they were, waiting by the double doors.

"You okay, D?" Janie asked, wide-eyed.

"I'm straight. He's gonna make it so that's all that matters to me," I said nonchalantly.

"Everything gonna be alright, y'all," Jamal said with a shaky voice. He just wanted to say something to ease the tension because Jamal barely talked anyway.

At lunch, the three of us sat in silence. They probably felt a little guilty about that day, but I wasn't trippin' and I decided to let it out. "I'm glad y'all decided to go home because ain't no telling what would have happened. I know that you guys feel like you did something wrong but naw, things would have gone south either way and... I'm glad that y'all here right now because I need my homies right now. I love you guys, forreal," I said with tears in my eyes.

"Whatever you need bro, we gotchu," Janie said, giving me a hug. Jamal joined in and at that moment, all the acting tough and hard in front of people ended. I cried in Janie's arms.

At first, we heard a few laughs from other students, then a few, "Shut the hell up—his friend got shot!" speeches. Then just complete silence. Either people decided to be quiet or my mind completely shut off in that moment. It just felt good being in my friend's arms, letting out a good cry. Sometimes we needed to cry. We had to let it out.

After crying in Janie's arms, I looked up and everybody was either looking at me or looking down with expressions of care and empathy. They understood and that meant a lot to me.

"Man, can we go visit him today or is that gonna be a problem?" Jamal asked.

"Naw, his mom told my mom that we can see him before seven today," I said.

"Cool, because I made some of my special cupcakes. My own recipe and I know he's going to like it," Jamal said, rubbing his hands together like he was Birdman.

I just hoped that Mickey didn't feel pissed about them not coming to the bando with us. I hoped that he could see that it was a blessing that they didn't join us in the first place.

When third block came around, we were kind of back to our regular selves making side comments, telling jokes, and texting each other funny things that happened in class. I was kinda glad things were getting a little better, but I was still a little shaken up. When the bell rang, my English teacher told me she wanted to talk to me after class. I knew the convo was going to be about Mickey.

"Deon, I know it's hard to see things like that happen and if you need anybody to talk to maybe you should go see a therapist. The school will pay for it and everything," she said with a concerned look.

I was confused. It sounded like she was trying to say I was crazy. "Look, I don't need no therapy! I ain't crazy!" I said defensively.

"Deon, you don't have to be crazy to see a therapist. I saw a therapist. Actually, I still do," she replied.

I was more confused than ever now. *My teacher went to therapy?* She was a sophisticated, intelligent black woman. Maybe she was lying. Maybe she wasn't. "Why do you need a therapist? You seem fine to me," I said.

Her look said, *Boy, you got a lot to learn.* "Deon, I'm not perfect, I have a lot of things going on in my personal life and sometimes you need somebody to hear you out other than your friends to give you a better perspective on your life," she said. She handed me a card and told me that if I ever decided to take the next step, to call the number and the school would take care of the rest. I told her thanks and went to my next block.

Janie and Jamal's mom volunteered to take us to the hospital after school, so I just walked with them to their house. I had always liked the Walters. They were an example of an actual black family that would be in a sitcom or something. The only difference was that their mom and dad were both blue-collar workers. Still, they didn't live in the hood and could live peacefully in their neighborhood. I wished the placc where I lived was like that. If I made it as an adult with a good career, I wanted a big house. Damn near a mansion if that was possible.

I sat in the living room, watching TV with Janie while Jamal was in the kitchen with his mom. Their dad was in the back room, asleep. Their living room was filled with pictures of the family and personal achievements on a table next to the sofa I was sitting on. Janie sat in the La-Z-Boy chair which was considered their dad's chair, but she was a daddy's girl and her dad didn't mind her sitting on the chair as long as he wasn't there. The AC was on which made the house pretty chill. It was a pretty good environment to be in and I could see why Janie and Jamal decided not to come to the traphouse. A lot was at risk for them. They didn't live like us; they lived a little better and were in a two-parent household. They had a system that was loving and rooted in good decisions which explained why they didn't come with us that night.

"Cupcakes are almost ready. Should we get a card or balloons?" Jamal asked.

I reached in my pocket and pulled out a folded piece of paper. "This is a poem that I wrote for him," I said.

Janie smiled in approval and pulled out a piece of artwork. It was a beautiful and creative heart with blue skies in the background. The girl was very talented.

"That's so dope, Janie!" I said. Out of anything, Mickey was going to like that. I hope he liked my poem as well.

After Jamal finished the cupcakes, he gave each of us one for a sample. He said it was a chocolate, caramel, cheesecake cupcake and to me that seemed like a bit much. Janie looked excited. I guess she was just used to it and already knew how they tasted.

"They betta be good, Jamal," I said, taking one.

"Man, they outa this world. Betta believe it," he said with confidence.

I took one bite of the cupcake and my whole world changed. I felt like heaven was calling my heart. It was literally the best thing I'd ever eaten. "Daaaaammmnnn bro, this sh-" I stopped because I remembered his mom was in the same room but she just started laughing.

He nodded several times as if to imply that he knew his cupcakes were bomb.

"Man, he's gonna love these, oh my God!" I said.

His mom held up the keys which indicated it was time to go. It was time to see my bro.

•••

The ride to the hospital was pretty quiet. We listened to nineties R&B which made the ride comfortable. I loved old school music from the nineties. New Edition was my favorite.

Their house was about seven minutes from the hospital, so it didn't take long. After we parked, everyone got out and waited for Mrs. Walters to lead the way. Jamal had a smile on his face, anticipating Mickey's response to his cupcakes. I was not smiling. I don't know how he would react to Janie and Jamal or even me. Would he blame me for getting shot? It was time. As we approached the entrance doors, my heart began to pound.

Inside the hospital, it was the same scene as always. Some people were sick, some were injured, some looked like they were waiting on the news, some were sleeping, and others were in the waiting room for support. We didn't even take a seat. We skipped the process and talked to the receptionist. She called the nurse and the nurse gave us the okay. Now it was *really* time. Walking down those hallways and through the double doors made me nervous but it could also just have been excitement for seeing my homie.

Mrs. Walters walked in Mickey's room first and the rest of us followed; I was the last one. When we walked in, the nurse said, "Hey Mickey, you have some visitors." When Mickey saw us, a big smile appeared on his face. He was very happy to see us.

"My dawgs, what's up? Man, I'm happy to see you guys," he said, pulling his head up a little. Mrs. Walters asked the nurse if it would it be alright for her to step out. The nurse was fine with that. When Mrs. Walters stepped out, we loosened up a little.

"Mickey man, we're sorry. We should have been there for you, no matter what," Jamal said, still holding the cupcakes.

"Bro, you and Janie were right. You don't be around that type of stuff so why would you come?

Plus, me and D didn't know that would happen. It came from nowhere. I'm just glad you guys weren't there because if you would have gotten shot, I would have felt guilty and couldn't live with myself," Mickey said sincerely.

Jamal and Janie were glad for the reassurance that Mickey wasn't pissed off and was regular old Mickey.

"When will you be gettin' outta here, bro?" I asked.

"In a couple of days. I'm glad I'm getting a break from school. I ain't complaining one bit," he said.

We all laughed. Yep, my boy was back. Jamal took out a cupcake and told Mickey to try it. Mickey took it reluctantly and started examining the cupcake like he was a food inspector. "This the famous cupcakes you been raving' about bruh?" he asked.

Jamal simply nodded his head with a smile, waiting for Mickey to take a bite. Mickey took a bite and immediately tossed the cupcake at the wall across the room! Jamal looked disappointed and Janie, the nurse, and I looked surprised.

"Bro, what the hell?" he said, looking at Jamal somewhat angrily.

"What, you didn't like them?" Jamal asked, looking concerned.

Mickey sat up a little. He looked at each of us one by one with the same angry look and then fixated on Jamal again. "I just wanted to cause a scene because I assume the rest of those are mine—but that is hands down best I ever had, bro, real talk."

We all laughed. We should have known that Mickey was up to his usual tricks. He was always doing something like that. Jamal was very happy and proudly placed the cupcakes on the table next to Mickey's bed. Next, Janie and I gave him the art piece and the poem. I was interested to see how he would react to the poem because as soon as he looked at the painting, he smiled wide-eyed at Janie, signaling it was dope. He unfolded the sheet of paper with my poem and read it aloud.

WHO IS MICKEY
Who is Mickey?
I'm the last man standing
when at war, the last man to die.
When truly hurt, the first real man not afraid
  to cry.
I live for today because tomorrow may not come
So, who am I? I'm the bullet inside the gun.

The passion I have for life is all from my
*   heart*
I never wait until the end to fight—I fight
*   from the start.*
You can talk about me until the day I die
Cause I really truly don't know who am I.

After reading it, his eyes looked puffy, and he looked like he was holding back tears. "That was dope, man. Thanks to the both of y'all, forreal. You know I been thinking about leaving all this street life behind me. Maybe it ain't worth it like I thought it was. I got to go to my cousin's funeral in a couple of days. I don't want y'all to come to mine next," he said.

We all nodded and understood what he was saying. We had to be there for him to make that transition if he wanted to stay clean and get off the streets for good. That meant we had to help him change his mindset because all of this crap we dealt with was psychological anyway.

"Before you guys go, you remember that bookbag I had on, D?" he asked.

"Yeah, I believe it's still locked up in your car," I replied.

"I need you to give it to Ricky for me, bro, and I'll handle the rest when I get out. I know I'm asking for a lot but in order for me to get out of this life, I have to start there first."

"I gotcha bro, I'll go get it right now," I said.

"Naw, take an Uber here and back tomorrow. That smell might be ridiculous," he said.

I gave him a fist bump, signaling that I had him. We all gave him love and then left soon after.

•••

After getting dropped off at home, I started to think about the pressures we put on ourselves and why we tended to do the things we did. It seemed like we wanted validation from others to the point that we started to lose ourselves. I decided we should forget other people's approval, and start living for ourselves. Better ourselves. "The Marathon Continues," as Nipsey Hussle would say. That meant run your own race and treat it like a marathon.

That night reminded me that I needed to focus on myself first. People often tended to get mad and become envious and jealous of the person who was running in front of them because that person was either living their purpose, taunting others behind them, or getting cheers from the crowd that they thought they deserved. Being envious of such a person was wrong because that person was not running the envious person's race. He or she was on the same track—the journey of life. However, everyone was running their own race. We should run at our own pace in life and become the persons *we* want to be and not succumb to the pressures to become who everybody else wants us to.

I lay in my bed, took out my notebook and started to write another poem. This one was going to be for the contest.

POEM FOR COMPETITION (NO NAME YET)
The evolution of the black man in America,
tell me who can make this man a man again,
standing there frozen like a mannequin,
see his tongue sits there at the edge of his gut
swallowed and absent from pride
we were all taught that a man's pride is all
  he has
so why is it at this moment in space, pride is
  motionless from my face
as tears stream like you never seen
a celebrity on Ustream, you scream cause it
  feels good,
It's my way of crying in public without losing
  all masculinity,

while embracing the insanity of the little boy
  stuck inside of me.
See this little boy is tired of seeing these
  bullets bounce like 6x4s.
This girl was six years old and won't make it
  to see seven,
climbing the stairs of heaven, shot and killed
  by a dirty reverend...
how ironic.

6

Mission Impossible

The next morning, I decided to skip my first block so I could retrieve Mickey's bookbag from the car. I had to do it early in the morning before the police started their rounds of harassment and before the gangsters and such started to activate. Around twelve was when things usually started to happen so I had to hurry up and get this thing done and be ready for my second block that started at 9:15. Technically I had time, but then again, I didn't.

My mom came home and went straight to sleep after her shift, so I didn't have to worry about her being all over my back, even though she didn't do that anyway. My Uber ride came around 8:15 a.m. He was a little weird, but I didn't care. I was on a mission.

"Hey bro, where you from?" he asked.

"Here," I said, looking out the window. He could see I was trying to avoid conversation, so he stopped talking and kept driving.

After seven minutes, I was by Mickey's car ready to retrieve the bookbag, but the front passenger window had been broken and his bookbag was gone! Somebody had robbed him. Maybe the guys who robbed him had found out where he kept his drugs but that was impossible. Who could have known about the bookbag? Whoever decided to break in had to have known. That was nothing new. Or maybe it was the cops. Maybe the cops broke into the car and were waiting for someone to come back to the car to arrest them! Or maybe I was just paranoid.

I still had to tell Mickey, though. This would shatter his entire world because he probably had to pay that money back to somebody like Ricky. I hurried to the hospital because I still had to get to my second block. I went to the receptionist and asked if I could see Mickey, but she was reluctant to let a fifteen-year-old head back there alone. I decided to sneak in because I knew exactly where his room was—I just had to be sly about it. I waited for the receptionist to go back to reading her book. As soon as she was preoccupied and seemed very much into the novel that she was reading, I slid back. Now the only thing I had to worry about was the security guard.

A heavyset security guard was sitting in a chair in the hallway, reading a magazine without a care in the world. He thought I was a family member, so he just glanced at me and let me go about my business. I was surprised he didn't ask, "Hey kid, why aren't you in school?" or something like that. I knocked on the door quietly and luckily the same nurse from the other day opened it. She was reluctant to let me in so she looked at Mickey for approval who gave her the nod to go ahead. I was surprised that he was awake. But then again, he was used to being up early for school.

"What's up, D? Got it done already?" he asked in surprise.

"Somebody took it, bro," I said, with my hands in my pockets.

"WHAT YOU MEAN SOMEBODY...?" he started yelling until he remembered he was in a hospital room. "Look bro, my mom just went to go get breakfast for us and then I might be out of here later this evening. But when I get out, meet me at the spot," he said with a very serious look on his face.

"I gotcha, bro," I replied. I gave him the deuces and then left. I wished I could have texted him all of this but he couldn't find his phone and might have to buy a new one. Next time, I'll definitely text him. I felt like Gee Money on *New Jack City* when Pookie sabotaged the Carter. I went to the front of the hospital and requested an Uber. Just my luck, the same weird driver who'd brought me came back around and picked me up. *Great.*

•••

When I got to school, I made it in time for second block. I would have to answer a lot of questions and didn't know where to start. At lunch, Janie and Jamal asked me if everything had gone smoothly. I just told them the truth about what had happened.

"It has to be somebody he knows. It's somebody from Ricky's crew," Janie said. She could be right because news did travel fast. I didn't know what to believe.

"You know what, maybe his mom did it," suggested Jamal.

"Shut up," Janie and I said.

"His mom would have called my mom and I would have been punished by now if that had happened," I added.

"Yeah and our mom would have told us that we can't hang around with him no more, boy," said Janie. He shrugged and went on eating his lunch.

As we sat at the lunch table, my mind started to wander. I was tired of living like this. I was not cut out for this kind of lifestyle. This stuff just needed to stop. Janie finished her lunch and then threw what was left in the trash.

"You know D, we should go ahead and get started with ideas for this poetry contest, don't you think?" she asked.

"Yeah, true, true," I said. She was right. The poetry contest was twenty days away and we had to practice. That's not a lot of time to prepare for something of this magnitude so today, we were going to have to start committing to practice. I wasn't trying to look stupid. Janie already took the liberty of signing us up anyway, so I had no choice. This was also a statewide contest to win a scholarship to any art school of our choice. This was a shot to set out on a new journey.

• • •

After school, Janie walked to my apartment since my mom wasn't home and we could have the place to ourselves to practice. Jamal went home to help his mom with a catering order. The walk was quiet. We were the type of people that could walk in silence without it being awkward. We always liked to think about innovative things. That's why we were such good friends and got along so well.

When we got to my place, we set our bookbags down and start getting out our materials. I got out my notebook and she pulled out her drawing pad.

"So, what should we talk about?" she asked.

"How about pain?" I said.

"What about healing?" she said.

"How about both?" I offered.

She nodded her head. "Let's get started. But before we do, let's talk about the things that hurt us."

"You first," I said, holding my hands up.

"Okay, that's cool." Putting her head down, she said, "When I was little, I got molested by my uncle."

I was shocked. "Wow, I bet your parents were upset," I said.

"Yep. When my mom and dad found out, my dad beat up my uncle and had him arrested. After he went to jail, he got out a year later. He says he learned his lesson from the last visit from my dad but... he shouldn't have done that period. That's why I am the way I am now. So closed in. So scared to be a girl," she said.

Hearing Janie say all these things and confessing was new to me. I hadn't known about the pain she'd been hiding. I felt bad for her but was also glad that she was strong enough to tell me and trusted me with this information.

"You still my bestie," I said, smiling at her. She smiled back. My turn.

"When I was younger, I had a little brother. Well, technically, I would have had one. The man that my mom was seeing at the time was pretty abusive and... he used to beat on her a lot. He claimed he loved her, but I didn't see it. How can you hurt someone you love? I never understood that." I swallowed hard and continued. "When my mom began to show, he used to turn up the beatings and one day he went overboard, and my mom lost her baby. He punched her twice in the stomach. Right in front of me. He was drunk and angry that night. I just wish I could have protected her," I said.

"How old were you?" Janie asked.

"Six," I responded.

We both sat in silence for about a good five minutes. I guess we both were feeling pain at that moment. We'd probably never told anybody about this until now. After that, we started getting to work and began writing and drawing. I ran to my room and got out my Bluetooth speaker. I went on YouTube and typed in "motivational music" and played a two-hour video.

"Yo, that's crazy that I'm not the only one that likes listening to this music!" Janie said, surprised.

"Yeah, it helps me concentrate," I said, smiling.

After two hours of working on our poem and painting, we decided to call it a night. It was only 6:30 but I wanted her to get back home before seven. After all the craziness that had gone on, I didn't want either of us to end up in a situation like the one with Mickey.

On the walk home, Janie pulled out her phone and grinned when she saw a text.

"Okay, who's the new dude?" I asked.

She laughed and answered, "You know RJ, the wide receiver? He asked me for my number at the party."

"You like him? Does he offer good convo?"

"Only thing he does is text 'what're you doing' and then we just go back and forth about what we did that day, but he's a very short texter."

"That's good, I guess. Do you see yourself with him?"

"I don't know. Maybe, we will see."

"I've never had a true girlfriend," I said.

"I've never had a true boyfriend, either."

The rest of the walk was pretty quiet. My respect for her had gone up tremendously. It seemed like every time I had alone time with her, I became more impressed with how strong she was, how beautiful she was and how... wait a minute, she was my friend. She the homie. I was trippin'.

As she went up the steps to her house, she asked me if I'd like to do the same thing, same time tomorrow. I said yeah, then we did our signature handshake and I was out.

On the walk home, I got a text from Mickey. He wanted me to meet him at the spot in fifteen minutes, so I redirected myself and started walking to the spot.

By the time I got to the spot, I saw Mickey pulling up. Mickey bumped music in his car before getting out. His window was still busted, and I knew he was upset about that. The music stopped and he stepped out of the car. He was wearing a Champion jogging suit and it looked like he had a bunch of padding on underneath protecting his wounds. He started pacing for a couple of seconds and then started talking.

"You know what's crazy? We were the only people that made it out of that house alive. I lost my cousin and a few friends there. I have to go to my cousin's funeral on Friday, bro. My mom wants me off the street, but she doesn't realize this lifestyle is what keeps the lights on at home," Mickey explained. "I lost all of my money and product. I feel like all of this is my fault. I could have worked faster. I could have invited my cousin to *my* house instead and everybody would have been safe. I hate my life!" he screamed, as tears poured down his cheeks.

I felt his pain and I knew he was upset so I had to choose my words carefully. "You gonna get through this, bro. We made it out! Either way, it was going to happen. It's not yo fault, not my fault, not yo cousin's fault, shit just happened, bro. You can't fault yourself for that. They were scheming. If not there, it would have been at your momma's house. Ever thought about that? They planned this, bro," I said.

He agreed and wiped his face. He started talking about how he'd met up with Ricky and how this past week, the crew got ambushed. Ricky told him that eleven people were killed, and Mickey was lucky not to be the twelfth. He told me that Ricky would spot him the re-up money under one condition— when the crew found out who actually killed his cousin and his friends in that house, Mickey would have to retaliate. He already knew that I wouldn't agree with that, so he said it in a nonchalant way to show me that he wasn't interested in doing something like that.

"Lowkey, though. I gotta make my money back so I'm about to ask Ricky to front me something. I promise this is going to be the last time," he said.

"Okay, bro. I believe you," I said, giving him a fist bump. After that, he dropped me off at home and drove off.

7

Write Way to Heal

The next morning, I met up with my friends back at the spot. Everyone was accounted for except for Mickey.

"Are we good to work on our little project today?" Janie asked.

"Yeah, for sure," I answered.

Jamal took out a notebook and started skimming over some notes. I figured that he had a test today because he was very engaged.

As Janie and I talked about ideas for our project, Mickey walked up to us.

"Where's your car?" I asked.

"My mom's putting it in the shop. Technically, it's hers anyways." Mickey then pulled out an airplane bottle of liquor. We didn't say anything. We knew that he was in pain and needed to get things off of his mind. I was concerned for my friend at that moment. He'd been through so much, and I hoped that he could break that cycle.

"I know this is wrong but just let me get my drink on for today, celebrating life and hanging with my homies. Thanks D, for saving my life and thanks Jamal and Janie for having my back and visiting me when I needed it most. This is my last shot and I'm done with drinking, smoking and all that stuff, man," he said.

I understood and didn't say anything else. We couldn't control what anyone did or thought so it was best to let him get through what he needed to get through.

At school, I saw Janie and her new friend talking in between classes and lunch. He was kind of all over her. Not physically but just chattering a lot. At the end of the school day, while we were walking back to my house, I decided to ask her about what was going on.

"He came over and... we did some things."

"Like...?"

"I lost my virginity," she confessed.

When she said that, my heart dropped. They hadn't been talking for that long. How? I'd wondered why he was so close and why she'd started to dress up more and look more girly instead of like a tomboy. All for that clown. I remained quiet for about five minutes and she noticed.

"D, what's wrong?" she asked.

"Nothing," I replied firmly, ending the conversation.

When we got to my apartment, I took out my notebook and started writing. I didn't say one word. I was livid, to be honest. I guess she got tired of the silence and started asking questions about the poem I was writing for the contest. I simply looked up at her and kept writing.

"D, you mad at me?" she asked.

"Nope, you do what you do, ya know. If you want to lose your virginity, then that's on you." She heard the hostility in my voice and started laughing hard. I started to get pissed. She didn't seem to care one bit about how I felt.

"Deon, I ain't have sex with that boy," she said. I immediately felt relieved to hear that.

"I ain't havin' sex until I'm an adult and I know the guy is going to marry me," she said, folding her arms.

"Wishful thinking. We're already grown anyway. Shoot, I'm the man of the house so I'm already an adult," I replied.

She looked at me with a frown and shook her head. "Boy, you ain't grown. You ain't payin no bills yet. That's when you grown," she said.

"Naw, I disagree."

"How come, D?"

"Because I'm independent. I'm on my own, basically. Got to do a lot of stuff by myself, Janie," I said, defensively.

"But you don't do everything by yourself. You don't pay bills."

"When I start working, I will. I'm getting a job this summer. Watch."

"D, focus on your goals and your dreams. You want the best for your mom so stop trying to give her a city when you can give her the world. Life is a marathon, not a sprint," Janie said. "I know you and your mom struggle but like Nip says, you have to avoid the fast money and let the marathon continue." I could not disagree with Janie on that one. She was a good friend.

Next week was the preliminary round of the contest so we started to practice the routine we would be doing on stage.

"This girl was six years old and won't make it to see seven, climbing the stairs of heaven, shot and killed by a dirty reverend...how ironic. As her soul shifts like tectonic plates, building mountains of hate, living in a world where love is too late because we value chase instead of the wait. Wait, so where is this evolution of the black man anyway? Have we even evolved at all? The question of this dissertation."

As I finished reciting my poem, including the new lines, Janie was just putting the finishing touches on her painting and our chemistry was magical. *We can't lose*, I thought to myself.

"That was soooo good. Oh my God! People are going to love it," Janie said with a big smile.

I looked up at the time and saw it was 6:30, time to take her home. We got our bookbags and headed downstairs. As we walked down the block, a spotless Infiniti SUV stopped in the street, idling next to us. The tinted window on the front passenger side opened. The driver was bald and wore shades and reminded me of the actor, Terry Crews, from the movie *White Chicks*.

"Ricky wants to see you," he said from the driver's seat.

Puzzled, I wondered what Ricky wanted to see me for. Was it because I'd been involved in the incident at the bando? Was it because he thought that I snitched or something? "What does he want?" I asked.

"Just meet him Sunday at one, no questions," he responded. The SUV pulled away.

"Damn, dude didn't even tell you where Ricky lives," Janie said.

"I know where he lives. I was there once with Mickey," I replied.

"Are you scared, D?"

"No, I'm not," I said unconvincingly.

"Then why are your hands shaking?" she asked.

My hands were shaking uncontrollably. Although I didn't want to say it, I was terrified. I decided to be straight up and tell the truth. "Yeah, can't even lie. Ima lil' shook," I said.

She took my hand. "I'm here for you, friend," she said. We walked all the way to her house, holding hands in silence. I felt safe, comfortable, and that everything would be okay.

"Same time tomorrow," Janie said, before going inside.

I saluted her and then walked back to my apartment with a little more confidence. That was a defining moment for us. I'd never felt like that before inside. I think I liked her. *Nah, that's the homie, I'm trippin*, I told myself.

When I get home, I lay in my bed and started to think about the meeting with Ricky. I thought about the poetry contest. I thought about Janie—a lot. I thought about Mickey and about why it seemed like he was losin' it instead of recovering. I didn't even know why but I thought about Jamal's cupcakes. Them cupcakes was *fye!*

I had a lot of things on my mind, but they appeared to give me enough inspiration to finish my poem for the contest. I took out my pen and pad and started writing.

•••

When I woke up Sunday morning, I realized the week had gone by fast and seemed like a blur. Janie and I had rehearsed our project. Jamal was in his own world because of a math and chemistry test. I hadn't seen or heard from Mickey all week except for on Thursday when he was at the spot and only said a few words to us. He was acting weird—I hoped he was alright.

I took a shower and started to relax a little. I know that it couldn't be that bad. They wouldn't try to kill me, right? After I got out of the shower, I headed to my room, dressed, and was on my way out the door. My mom was in the kitchen, cooking breakfast.

"Where you goin' this early? Usually you playin' that video game. Everything okay?" she asked.

"Yeah, I'm alright Mom. I'll be back around five maybe. Doing some work with Janie for our preliminary round tomorrow."

"Be safe," she said.

I was headed to the spot first to see Janie and Jamal and talk to them before my meeting with Ricky. Hopefully Mickey would show up, but the dude had not been himself this whole week.

When I arrived, nobody else was there yet. It was only 10:30, so I understood. I just stood there waiting, listening to soul music from the eighties. I liked listening to the old school stuff, it was very relaxing. Around eleven, Janie and Jamal showed up. Janie had on jean shorts, showing her beautiful long legs. Jamal was wearing the same black Tupac shirt that he wore weekly.

"You need us to come down there with you, D?" asked Janie.

"No, I'm good. This is something I need to do on my own," I replied.

"We got your back, no matter what," said Jamal.

I gave him a fist bump for saying that. I knew they had my back but the way that Mickey had been acting, I wonder if *he* had mine as well. I texted him but he did not even text back. I was worried and mad that he was a ghost in my time of need. I'd told him several times about my meeting with Ricky. He just kept telling me not to worry. Mickey was like a brother, but my concern was steadily growing that this could be a set up.

On my way to Ricky's place, I didn't ask anyone to come with me. I had to do this alone. To be honest, I just wanted to get this over with so I could go about my business. Ricky lived in a pretty nice cul-de-sac that kind of reminded me of Janie's neighborhood. A lot of people were hanging around outside, on the porch, and probably inside as well. Ricky was a popular leader and he wanted to make sure he was always protected. A whole bunch of guys wearing black jeans and tank tops were staring at me, but I didn't care. I walked up to the door and knocked.

"Go ahead and go in, Ricky expecting you," said this skinny guy standing by the door. I went in and Ricky and a bunch of guys were sitting at the table, eating wings and drinking. The chair beside Ricky was empty. I guessed that it was for me. A guy pulled the chair out and I sat while Ricky stared me down.

"What's up, lil bro, you doin' alright?" he said.

"Yeah, I'm doin' fine," I said, swallowing hard.

"Don't worry bro, you ain't in trouble, just got a proposition for you." He then pulled out a big bag of marijuana and put it on the table. "I heard what you did back at the bando and that you saved my lil' soldier Mickey from dying. Here's a gift," he said as he slid the bag to me.

I should take it; I should sell it and make some quick and easy money. This could help my momma out with the bills, I thought. "Yeah, Ima take it because our lights are about to get shut off—this is a gift, right?" I asked Ricky. Then I paused to think about Mickey's mistakes and Janie's advice.

Gently sliding the weed back to him, I said, "Naw, I'm fooling myself. Thanks Ricky, but I can't take this. I'm not a drug dealer. What I did was for my friend. I'm loyal to my friends."

He looked at the weed and then looked at me and started laughing and everybody else joined in. "Yo, you a good dude. I appreciate that comin' from a dude yo' age." He went in his pocket and gave me a handful of cash. "This for yo' momma light bill," he said, smiling.

When I got back to the spot an hour after I'd left, Janie and Jamal were still there. Still no sign of Mickey.

"You okay?" Janie asked, with a concerned look.

"Yeah, it was good. They have a lot of respect for me and what I did for Mickey. Have you heard from him?" I asked.

"Nope, no sign of him yet," Jamal chimed in.

I decided we should just rehearse at Janie and Jamal's house. From three to six, Janie and I performed our piece over and over and over again until it was perfect. Jamal was in and out, watching us perform while baking his special red velvet cupcakes.

"Let me take about four of these home with me?" I asked, as I watched him put on the finishing touches.

"Sure," he said, as he got out two paper plates and the aluminum foil.

When I got home, I shared two cupcakes with my mom.

"How was your day?" she asked.

"It was good. Got something else for you," I said, and handed my mom the cash Ricky had given me.

She looked perplexed but grateful and accepted the money. "Where did you get this?" she asked with a shaky voice.

"From a friend. I did a favor for him. Nothing illegal, Mom—trust me. I know better," I said confidently.

"Well, keep forty dollars for yourself," she said with a smile and tears in her eyes.

I gave her a long hug. "We gon' be straight momma, believe me."

Around nine, while I was playing the game, I started to daydream about how tomorrow would go. I turned the game off and lay in bed. *I told Janie I was the man of the house*, I thought, as I fell asleep.

8

The Ultimate Win

Today was the state competition. I got up and took a quick hot shower. My mom didn't have to work until tonight, so she would take me to the competition, and I would meet Janie there. Since the contest started on a Monday, we had both received excused absences from the school, which was cool. I put on my black suit, the only one in my closet. My mom bought it during my freshman year. It was big on me then, so it fit pretty good now.

"You ready, D?" Mom asked.

"Yeah, I am," I replied confidently.

The auditorium we were going to was located downtown and often held plays, musicals, and concerts. *This was going to be like a sophisticated talent show,* I thought to myself. When we arrived, people in red suits who looked like valets were standing behind a table. People around us were dressed up, laughing and smiling. A food bar served cheese, veggies, fruits, and drinks.

"What's the name of the participant?" a skinny white guy in a red suit asked me.

"Deon Sanders."

"Ohhh, like the football player, huh."

"No, I'm a poet," I replied.

"Okaaaaaay... gotcha. Here's your tags, don't lose them," he said, handing me our name tags to put on our shirts. "Hope you do well."

"D!!!" I heard my name being called by someone in the crowd. It had to be Janie. I turned to look for her. She looked so gorgeous. She wore a black dress with complementing white heels. She was wearing some makeup but not a lot, which I liked.

"You ready?" I asked.

"Of course—you?" she asked, smiling.

"Of course!" I said. "Hi, Mrs. Walters." Janie's mom greeted me, then the moms greeted one another and started talking.

"Janie and I are going over here to practice," I informed them, stepping to an area with less people. They said okay and continued their conversation as we walked to the other side of the lobby.

"Have you heard anything from Mickey?" I asked.

"No, I haven't. Hope he's doing okay," she said.

"I hope so too."

"Okay, let's run through this." We went through our plan about ten times, then suddenly our moms came running over to us.

"What's wrong?!" Janie and I asked.

"I don't know if we should tell you two until you are finished," said my mom, hesitantly.

"Go ahead, we can take it," said Janie, glancing at me quickly.

"Mickey's mom called. He has been detained by the police for suspicion of murder," she said with tears in her eyes.

He'd told me he wouldn't do it. He told me he was going to let it go! I knew his pride wouldn't let him walk away. Inner-city black kids like us needed pride to help us survive. Unfortunately, Mickey's misguided pride might have cost him his life.

"That's sad. But he made that choice," Janie said coldly.

"That's messed up, Janie," I responded.

"No, it's not. He knows better. He made a choice that he didn't have to make. He kept saying he wanted to get out of the streets but that was just talk!

That's the homie and all but you reap what you sow," she said with decisiveness.

I hated to agree but she was right. I'd tried with Mickey and he just hadn't listened, so he was going to have to pay the price for what he did.

"Let's go in and win this thing for our legacy," said Janie. We locked eyes, then I nodded, and we walked into the auditorium.

The show was about to begin. A woman in a blue dress came to the podium to introduce the contestants. "Welcome, everyone. This is the fifty-fourth annual Young Writers' Spirit Contest. The winner will receive a scholarship of their choice to any art school they decide to attend. So, let's begin!" she said. The audience applauded, then the contest got under way.

Over fifty contestants were competing in the event so we knew this would take a while. The first performer had written a short story, "Meow," about a cat morphing into a human being. The second one, a girl who looked bored and disinterested, read a boring poem on stage, which seemed to match her mood. The third one was pretty good; a cute biracial girl with long hair, wearing a blue dress read a pretty nice short story about a guy growing up with three friends. I enjoyed it a lot.

During her performance, we were backstage, anxiously waiting on our turn to take the stage. "It's our time," I said to Janie.

"Let's do this," she said, giving me a hug.

As we stepped onto the stage, the world seemed to stand still for a moment. The lights were bright, people were watching, and my heart was beating fast.

Janie's canvas was already set up. She took out her brushes and looked at me, waiting for my cue. Three...two...one. I closed my eyes briefly and let it out.

"The Evolved Black Man," I began. "The evolution of the black man in America—tell me who can make this man a man again, standing there frozen like a mannequin? See, his tongue sits there at the edge of his gut, swallowed and absent from pride. We were all taught that a man's pride is all he has so why is it at this moment in space, that pride is motionless from my face? As tears stream like you never seen a celebrity on Ustream, you scream 'cause it feels good. It's my way of crying in public without losing all masculinity, while embracing the insanity of the little boy stuck inside of me. See, this little boy is tired of seeing those bullets bounce like six by fours. This girl was six years old and won't make it to see seven, climbing the stairs of heaven, shot and killed by a dirty reverend...how ironic. As her soul shifts like tectonic plates, building mountains of hate, living in a world where love is too late because we value chase instead of the wait." I paused for a moment, scanning the audience.

"Wait—so where *is* this evolution of the black man anyway? Have we even evolved at all? The question of this dissertation. Or have we become complacent? And settled for adaptation? Adapting to the simple ways of a society gone astray, where we exchange Bibles for rifles with gangsters as idols, reproducing the cycle, where young black boys never tried to grow into men. Cause living in hoods, these bullets fly from brothers in black hoods, up to no good. Or are they simply Trayvon Martins, with Zimmermans marching, killing in self-defense? Hence... busting twenty-twos without a clue, cause all society can seem to do is find the *hood* inside of you."

After I finished, the crowd remained silent for a long moment, then burst into thunderous applause. I looked over at the picture that Janie had painted while I was reciting my poem. It was beautiful. Her painting was of an Anime guy with an afro holding a heart in his hands, looking toward the sky. Janie was smiling at me. *We won—I know we did!*

The rest of the contest was a blur. Nobody else particularly stood out and I knew we were going to win. The judges deliberated then made their decisions for first, second and third place. First place would win a scholarship, second would receive a $500 Visa gift card, and third would win Beats by Dre headphones. We only wanted the scholarship.

The woman in the blue dress returned to the stage to announce the winners. "The judges have added up the scores and we have our winners. But first I'd like to thank all of you wonderful students from so many different schools and counties for participating. Here we go!"

My heart was racing. Janie looked nervous. Our moms looked nervous. *Here we go.*

"Our third-place prize goes to Sandra Faried for her short story, 'Made in Heaven.'"

"That one was pretty good; good for her," I commented.

"Our second-place prize goes to Deon Sanders and Janie Walters for their poem and artwork compilation, 'Write Way to Heal.'"

When she called our names for second place, I felt like Kanye West at the VMAs. *Ours* was the best! I NEEDED that scholarship! Janie and I were in complete shock and disbelief. Our moms were cheering and happy for us, but we all knew we should have won first place. I guess they were looking at the bright side—at least we won something, right?

"Our first-place winner is... Kayla Rodgers for her poem, 'Green Pastures Arise.'"

What the hell? That boring girl that performed before us? *We* should have won. Our moms knew it too and probably everybody in the building as well! I held my head up high. At least I can say I pushed myself today.

After accepting our prize, we left the auditorium and went back out to the lobby. Everybody was talking and congratulating each other. I looked around, trying to find the girl who had won so I could congratulate her.

"You looking for that girl, ain't it," Janie stated.

"You know me well," I said with a smile.

"Well, just to let you know," she said, "we did great and you opened up my mind to poetry, art, and just being positive. Deon, I just want you to know that even though we did not win the competition, we won something bigger today."

"And what's that?"

"We learned that in spite of our circumstances and environment, we can be something other than an athlete or rapper. Hundreds of people were screaming for us on that stage, and it was because of how well we used our minds, not our bodies. You showed me something different and I thank you for that," said Janie, as a single happy tear rolled down her beautiful, brown cheek.

"Well, I'm glad I could do that for you, Janie," I replied, nervously.

"Why the weird look, Deon? Do you have something to say?"

"Yeah," I replied, with a grin.

"Well, what?" she asked.

"You are beautiful, you are amazing, and... I *like* you like you," I said in a shaky voice.

Janie looked at me, wrinkling her nose in disgust, and took a deep breath as if she were about to hurt my feelings even if she didn't want to. Then she smiled and grabbed my hand. "Well, it's about damn time! Because I like you too."

The End

Deon's Journal

Every poem in this book was written based on actual situations and events. Although they were fit into the context of this fictional story, they were inspired by real life experiences of the authors, Josh and Rodrekous. So, enjoy the poems in their raw, uncut form.

How Can You Judge Me

How can you judge me without knowing the person
that's within

How can you categorize me by the color of my skin

Why would you degrade me, how could you tell
those lies

Why do you envy me because of the color of my eyes

What's wrong with me, why am I the scum of the earth

And why does it seem as if I've been cursed since birth

What do I have to do so that I can be treated like
a human

Why do you judge me by how I look rather than what
I'm doing

You judge me out of the womb; you hated me out of
the uterus

I was still a child, life—I was new to it.

Yet you judge me, you even took me from my land,
said to me over and over, I would never be a man

But we still rose as a people, walking hand and hand,
finishing with the words of Barack Obama saying,
YES WE CAN!

Who Am I?

Who am I?

I'm the last man standing

when at war, the last man to die.

When truly hurt, the first real man not afraid to cry.

I live for today because tomorrow may not come

So, who am I? I'm the bullet inside the gun.

The passion I have for life is all from my heart

I never wait until the end to fight—I fight from
the start.

I never give in to self-defeating thoughts

How could I when I am the lion in the jungle?

I've mastered the arrogance of life while still
remaining humble

You can talk about me until the day I die

'Cause I really truly don't know who am I.

Until Death Do Us Part

Until death do us part
I promise you my heart.
I promise you my best
within my heart, you be my guest.
I think about you every day
yet I still can't find the words to say.
When I tell you I love you, it's truly from my heart
And I promise to feel that way...till death do us part.

Life's Changes

As that time slowly approaches, I hear life's changes knocking at my door

I promise to never forget those that I love and adore

Pressured by time and the decisions I have to make

Fear of giving life my all because of the losses I may take

Yet I extend my hand and welcome life's changes with a smile

'Cause I'm committed to being successful, I'm willing to go the extra mile

Despite the changes that life has for me, I promise to stay at ends

I will always keep my promises and stay true to true friends

I promise myself to be a good judge of what's wrong and what's right

I will never ask why this had to happened on that night

'cause I fully understand it's just the changes of life.

Congruent Minds

Two different people living on the same lines
we both live for the future, yet we stay looking behind
we fight and agree, yet we stay dry during the rain
we're separated only by death and become closer
through the pain
we walk, talk, laugh, and cry, all of one accord
we win every battle, fighting with the same sword
we climb mountains together, we breathe at the
same time
congruently speaking, you can say we're one of a kind
or just two different lovers with the same
congruent mind.

A Poor Man's Cry

Before my mom had the finances to birth me, I was already born economically cursed, cursed since my poor, innocent birth

Sixteen years and yet I'm a living recession

Many blessings, still—I AM the great depression

Should I hang my head low? And wallow in my poverty?

Give in to the devil's grief and lose all sovereignty?

Should I just throw in the towel and use my financial disability as a crutch?

Cause the weight of the world is on my shoulders and it just weighs too much.

I could do all of these things but instead I will stand tall

I will get up like a man, no longer will I crawl

They say you can tell a lot from a man whose back is against the wall...

Well here I am devil—put on ya gloves, it's time to brawl

You may think I'm weak but I'm not gonna die

These are simply just my thoughts, a poor man's cry.

I Wonder Why

I wonder why there's 365 days in a year

I wonder why out of sadness flows a tear

I wonder why some people portray an image that's
not within themselves

I wonder why life is just the preparation for death

I wonder why God smiles on the earth when people
so wrong

I wonder why you have to be weak before you can
be strong

I wonder why doing wrong is soo much easier than
doing right

I wonder why the sun makes day, and the moon
only night

To look for these answers is what I shall not try

So, the question will always linger, I wonder,
I wonder why...

No Pain

I have no pain, my tears don't flow

I have no sorrow; my pain does not grow.

Blessed is my soul, happy is my heart

I am who I am; my personality leaves a mark.

My body is strong, yet my mind exceeds that

I go opposite of the crowd; I lead from the back.

My eyes tell stories, my mind travels for miles

I go the extra distance; my expectations are above
the clouds.

I have no limits, I will exceed the skies

My mark will be forever, because I am God's Child.

Who Cares for Me

Who cares for me, when my heart is full of pain, my
 days full of rain, and I'm said to be insane

Who cares for me, when my legs are unable to walk,
 and my mouth unable to talk

When life has a gun to my head, who cares enough
 for me to come and set me free

Who cares for me when my back is against the wall,
 my problems are standing tall, and there is no one
 there to call

Who cares enough to cry for me, when my pain is
 beyond tears, and I'm unable to face my fears that
 have been haunting through the years

Who cares for me as I watch my grandma die, and
 all I can do is cry, while daily I'm saying goodbye

Who cares for this man who's walking, yet is lost?
The only one I know of died upon the cross.

Weak Man

His body is so weak, his eyes full of pain

My life has been so sunny, his full of rain

His face shows a smile, yet his heart is soaked with tears

He had to become a man while young, and was forced to face his fears

He's more than a man I know, he's stronger than what I see

He's really a strong man because that's what he had to be

Conversation Between
Love and Hate

Dear Love,

My name is Hate. I write to you today with a deep concern about the concepts of your beliefs, but first let me enlighten you of the simple beliefs I possess. From my own personal feelings, if you achieve more than I do, then I despise you because that should have been me. I hate everything that's not like me because it's not me! I hate living so close to you because you make all the visitors happy and smiling, and when they're done with you, they always come across the line to me crying and upset. That's why I always encourage murder so that all other feelings and emotions can stay far away from me. I despise anything that is not bad and anything that encourages happiness—that's why I hate you.

I don't understand how you, the almighty LOVE, can be perceived to be so good and I'm the one that no one wants to associate themselves with. People spend their whole life looking for you while at the same time running from me. I HATE YOU, LOVE! You live closer to me than anybody in this world yet the only time you converse with me is when you mess up and want one of your old friends back.

Nothing about you is real; I hold every piece of you in discontent. I don't understand how you let people do you so wrong, yet you still love and care for them. You're Stupid. I don't understand you; tell me something, anything, and I do mean anything.

With Great Aversion,
HATE

Dear Hate,

I hope this letter finds you in the best of health. I would like you to know that I sincerely feel where your concerns come from, and I do understand the magnificent hostility which you feel for me. Believe it or not, I too can relate to what you are going through. I have a cousin whose name is Lust, and people often use me just to get to Lust. How do you think that makes me feel? At least people come from me to you in search of comfort. People only come to me—LOVE—looking for my cousin Lust.

However, I don't fret, I stay where I am and continue to love. When all the pleasures of Lust are diminished, I will still be here. Something else you should understand is that I'm not a normal feeling. I'm a feeling from a higher power—God. That's how I continue to love and care when people do me wrong. I continue to love because loving is right. Hate will never solve anything, and love will last forever. I hope I have answered all your questions and concerns, and again—I hope all is well with you. With great love and respect, I write.

Sincerely,
LOVE

Knock Knock

Knock Knock, who's there? I'm here with no fear,
standing at life's college ready to matriculate, feeling
very articulate, my enemies must be sick of it,
but no no no, I stand alone wit my ambitions,
you haters are the keys and the fuel that ignites
my ignition
while you're heading towards omission, I slowly take
my position
to excel...take a deep breath and Exhale a full breath
while I'm swimming in a pool of great achievers,
in church praying desperately, surrounded by great
believers
Believers in God, believers in my confidence, trying
not to feel incompetent
While all along feeling heaven-sent, I'm persistent
so constantly I'm knocking at life's university,
knocking down all adversity
that's put in place to derail me,
but I stay on track cuz if I wanna be successful, Ima
have to do what I can
so knock, knock, life—here waits a man.

Is It Still True?

Is it still true that we are all inherently equal
when Sean Bell taking fifty shots to the chest is just
    another sequel
to the tragic death of Emmett Till
but still, we constantly bleed out of our mental,
    battling the vicious cycle,
clutching onto every dear word written in our
    precious Bibles,
as words blast off, piercing the soul like rifles
that are shooting down every dream and epiphany
    that's left in me
So tell me, is it still true that we can be whoever we
    wanna be
in this precious land of the free?
Or are we holding on to the lies 'cause we need
    something to believe
Is it still true that my father loves me,
though I'm nothing more than a memory in
    his brain,
instead of being a father, he fell in love with cocaine,
so who is there to blame? no one.
I just hope he comes around before life's clock
    stops ticking,
and my soul grows cold, and my heart stops wishing

So tell me—is it still true that U.S. Africans are Americans

when the road we're heading down is just leading to oppressed again

If not with chains from masters, then fathers without masters,

As they lower their degrees, getting further away from sons

by just packing up their lives and preparing to run

So let us scatter back to a time when all the skies were once blue,

when the flowers once grew...

and all the answers to these questions were all once TRUE.

Letter to Failure

As the light went on, and I illuminated the brain,
realizing you run synonymous with death like crack
and cocaine,
you run all around the earth in search for someone
else to blame,
someone else to hurt, and someone else to shame.
Though many times you succeed in turning the
strong into lame,
one thing you will never altar is the substance of
my brain.
I know that the sun is shining, even during the rain
and I remembered how to smile, even during the pain
because I realized what you're doing is nothing more
than a game
that many people have played but just couldn't
remain sane
long enough to know that a single loss does not
mean defeat
and the men who are strong, they too were once weak.
But I'm a different breed, cut from a different cloth,
failure can't stop me, I'll win at all cost
because over your set sidetracks, I'm prepared to be
your BOSS
cause I'm prepared for my next victory even before
my next loss.

Story Told Backwards

This is a story told backwards, like Kris Kross's
    hat was,
feeling salty like Atlas, spelled backwards, of course
living life in reverse, rolling backwards in a hearse,
    trying to figure what's worse:
leaving my grave, or heading towards my funeral,
    mind running in circles because everything's
    unusual
lying in this casket, I know everything coulda been
    so opposite
but everything ma told me to do, I chose to do the
    opposite
like "son go here," but instead I went there, which
    landed me in here—the hospital, that is—fighting
    and crying just trying to live,
thinking how I can't die young, I haven't had a
    chance to live
I should still be on the block with all my homies
    and friends
but bad decisions and good intentions got me
    traveling from the end
riding in the ambulance, life flashing before my eyes,
holding my girl's hand as I hear her silent cries
staring in this man's face with a mask as a disguise
BOOM!! was all I heard when I looked into his eyes

bullet wound to the chest,
fresh green grass is the place that I rest
I'm a good kid, should have never gotten shot or be
lying right here
didn't listen to what ma said so I'm not over there
right place, wrong time, so I'm lying right HERE!
at the intro of my outro, lying in my hazard
suffering the consequences of a story told
backwards!

Just Wasn't Meant to Be

See, I'm not even an ex but this X is feeling vexed

cause every message that I texted was just buried and put to rest

This is my pro- to your -test, for your love—not your pecks

and to break down all those walls that were built so complex

but instead, I rest. It just wasn't meant to be,

that now I..C..U.

L.O.V.E.

A friend once told me, "Love is an acronym meaning
  levels of valuable experiences," and I believed it.
Shit, I thought love was a goal and I went and
  achieved it
Turns out it wasn't love though; it was nothing more
  than a mere infatuation
for placing my heart in a safe destination
See, I can admit that I fall easy. I've told every girl I
  been with that she was the first girl I ever loved,
  the first girl I ever hugged and the first spark
  to my plug
The older I got, the more I realized how ridiculous
  this lie was
so I dropped the hug line and replaced with
  whatever and moved to the next like
"Baby, I never been in love but play ya cards right
  and be the spark to my plug,
the first girl I ever kissed an' the first girl I ever
  HUUU—*missed*!"
This is the poem all my boys told me NOT to write
but it's like I just can't seem to find that one Mrs.
  Compatible
so, I still write these in Mr. LL's practical.
I'm broke, my house burned down and I can't love—
  I'll explain before I proceed

cause indeed, I'll be clowned and detached from manhood and ran outa hoods for wanting true love and monogamy, but Jay-Z got B... and A.J. had Free.

Shoot, we even live in sin 'cause Adam loved Eve

so now you see why this is the poem all my boys told me not to write,

the poem about love and monogamy—as I search for it

like a crossword puzzle, I'm puzzled by the words I find in place of love

I seem to find words like lust or jealousy,

the complete opposites of what love is supposed to be.

I find confusion instead of clarity, selfishness instead of charity

and I find myself settling for good looks and stress instead of a God-fearing woman

with the strength of a lion but the spirit of an angel, who's as cute as an angle too.

So, I sit in this room once more, staring at this wall,

my conscious speaks again and says to me,

"Love—you have it every time you look in ya mom's eyes—it's there; or what about the look of tranquility and peace in the eyes of your niece when you hold her little hand and realize this is your brother's seed?

Indeed, love is there, like square to a box or a bucket to a mop or a shoe to a sock...

I'm sure you get the point. The point is that love is internal not some inferno that can be lit and dimmed upon request

Yes, the heart is in the chest, but love can't be rocked like a bulletproof vest

taking shots getting left by those that just weren't RIGHT

To love, learn to love God, then love yourself, and then family—all the rest will come."

As those words from my conscience trickled down my spine like two nickels from a dime, I stood there, indubitably in love with myself, God, and family

My conscience spoke, I guess I listened

You should too.

LOVE = Levels Of Valuable Experiences

Lebron James

I am king, not prince or president yet I still set
a precedent
ninety million dollars before I could even vote
for president
all this bragging, yes, its relevant
cause these critics want my head like a trial and
testament
this game is evidence to the world and all its
measurements
they seem to measure all the things that matter
the least
I dropped 40, 19, and 9 and all they focus on is 9
like "It's not triple double" yet my game is so potent,
they compare me to Michael and you mad cause
I'm closer?
What about the reality and these kids dying causally,
as you assassinate my greatness to boost your
freaking ratings
these kids are looking on as their hero's debated
see I told you I was king, not prince nor president,
yet I still set a precedent
ninety million dollars got my ma out that
predicament
ninety million dollars got my boys out the ghetto,
moved my family to the meadow,

as I play, you sit, and make noise like a cello—fellow,
   I hear you

and as I skip these bayless oceans, I relive my
   childhood through the screen as if I'm the curious
   case of Benjamin Button, living life backwards
   only to be judged by eyes full of love yet hearts full
   of envy, shooting bullets that won't hit me, and
   aiming for the kid that lives deep within me

This game is not a joke to me, it's been my therapy
   since poverty

so, I say these words cockily

I am king, not prince nor president yet I still set
   a precedent

ninety million dollars couldn't alter my judgment or
   alter my precession when I made the decision

I knew exactly what I was doing and the goal I was
   pursuing desired steady brewing

I consumed it like a customer—no, I consumed it
   like a schizophrenic boy fighting in Vietnam with
   a gun that's a toy

just shooting for the stars, I shot

and now I'm the star and everybody's shooting for
   me, a young black kid from Akron

I took the cards I was dealt and turned hell into
   the rapture

because I am king, not prince nor president. Yet I
   still set precedent

rich black teen with changing the world on my
    regimen and ever stronger on my mind
now eleven years later, that same world is mine! And
    I'm sure you wonder why?
Because for the last time, I AM KING
in a position I shall remain
cause I am the first and last LeBron James.

Your Turn

When Rodrekous and I began writing poetry, we both agreed we were just trying to escape the reality of our environment. Having both grown up poor and around crime, we saw it as our way to a better life. Poetry is all about self-expression. I wrote my first poem ever because I was mad at my teacher for sending me to in-school suspension. I probably deserved it, but I was angry, so I wrote about it. Poetry is about writing what you feel—it's that simple!

Try it for seven days and don't feel like you have to fill an entire page.

Only

Write

What

You

Feel

Your Poetry/Feelings Journal

DAY 1

_____

_____

_____

_____

_____

_____

_____

_____

_____

_____

_____

_____

_____

_____

_____

_____

_____

Your Poetry/Feelings Journal

DAY 2

_____

_____

_____

_____

_____

_____

_____

_____

_____

_____

_____

_____

_____

_____

_____

_____

Your Poetry/Feelings Journal

DAY 3

_____

_____

_____

_____

_____

_____

_____

_____

_____

_____

_____

_____

_____

_____

_____

_____

_____

_____

_____

Your Poetry/Feelings Journal

DAY 4

_____

_____

_____

_____

_____

_____

_____

_____

_____

_____

_____

_____

_____

_____

_____

_____

_____

_____

Your Poetry/Feelings Journal

DAY 5

_____

_____

_____

_____

_____

_____

_____

_____

_____

_____

_____

_____

_____

_____

_____

_____

_____

_____

Your Poetry/Feelings Journal

DAY 6

_____

_____

_____

_____

_____

_____

_____

_____

_____

_____

_____

_____

_____

_____

_____

_____

_____

Your Poetry/Feelings Journal

DAY 7

_____

_____

_____

_____

_____

_____

_____

_____

_____

_____

_____

_____

_____

_____

_____

_____

_____

_____

Write Way

Always remember—whatever your situation is in life, it's ALWAYS okay to write about it. Many teenagers turn to things that will only bring more harm to themselves and their families. So, the next time you're feeling any emotion—anxiety, sadness, excitement, love, or happiness—please understand that's a great time to write about it.

Write

What

You

Feel

About the Authors

Authors Rodrekous and Josh first met in college as roommates. They immediately became close friends, united by their similar childhood. Josh and Rodrekous both grew up as low-income inner-city kids. However, they used the power of their imagination to escape the reality of their environment. After meeting in college, they founded Coastal Carolina University's first ever PEACE Club (Performers Emerging Above Circumstances to Excel) to provide other students with a platform for expressing themselves. The organization went on to win multiple awards, including the NAACP's Organization on the Rise Award. Rodrekous currently serves as the President for Peace Nation, LLC, an independent record label designed to help local artists gain exposure. Josh is a teacher, football coach, and athletic director. He is also the owner of Rock Hill Video Company in Rock Hill, South Carolina. *The Write Way to Heal* is Josh's and Rodrekous's first published book.

Joshua Bovill

•

Rodrekous Hunter

•

Made in the USA
Las Vegas, NV
29 September 2021

31357442R00100